A DOCTOR'S
CHRISTMAS

LAURA SCOTT

READSCAPE PUBLISHING, LLC

❀ Created with Vellum

1

Pilot Megan Hoffman entered the Lifeline debriefing room, sweeping her gaze over the staff already seated at the table. Reese Jarvis was the off-going pilot and Ivan Ames, one of their paramedics, was seated beside Dr. Matthew Abbott, one of the emergency medicine residents. Flight nurse Kate Weber was also there, but there was a doctor missing from what she could tell.

Megan tried not to gag at the strong scent of coffee. She took a tentative sip of her chamomile tea she'd brought in from home as she took a seat beside Reese, praying her stomach wouldn't rebel.

"Clear day, no threat of snow." Reese Jarvis waved at the radar screen. "Just two weeks before Christmas and we still don't have any snow. So much for having a white Christmas."

Megan forced a smile. "Yeah, interesting that our first blizzard was the end of October. We've had a weird weather pattern, that's for sure. But I'm glad we have good flying conditions for the day."

Reese tipped his head to the side and frowned. "Are you feeling okay?"

Panic tightened her throat. "Yes, why?"

Reese shrugged. "I don't know, you look pale and tired. Maybe you need more sleep."

"I'm fine." She tried to hide the churning in her stomach. *Please don't throw up. Please?*

"Good morning." Dr. Drake Thorton entered the debriefing room wearing his navy blue one-piece flight suit that matched the ones they all wore, along with his usual serious, somber expression. He was handsome in a dark brooding way, if you were into that kind of thing. Thankfully, she wasn't. Of all the residents working this three-month rotation, Megan wasn't sure she'd ever seen Drake Thorton smile. He had issues, but didn't everyone? Frankly, she had enough problems of her own than to worry about his. "Who looks pale and tired?"

"No one." The last thing Megan wanted was for more attention to be focused in her direction. She glanced at Ivan, the paramedic coming off duty. "How's your daughter?"

"Great. Bethany is behaving much better now that we have Eddie the Elf watching her from the shelf." Ivan grinned. "Thank goodness for Christmas traditions."

Drake stiffened for a moment, then turned toward Matthew, the physician who'd been on the night shift working with Ivan. "Anything major happen last night?"

"Nah." Matt yawned widely and shrugged. "Overall quiet. Just a couple of transfers and the usual trauma calls. No significant events en route."

"Good." Drake gave a curt nod. "Let's hope that trend continues for the rest of the day."

"Agree." Megan swallowed hard, willing her stomach to settle down. She had a couple of cheese slices and saltine crackers in her bag, but she didn't want to eat them in front of the crew.

"Any pending transfers?" Kate asked.

"Nothing." Ivan shrugged. "Could be the calm before the storm though. The word from the CDC is that this year's flu is going to be a bad one."

Megan took another sip of her tea. Before she'd come to work at Lifeline as a chopper pilot, she hadn't believed the flu could actually kill people. But now she'd seen the impact firsthand, mostly the very young or the elderly, but even recently a twenty-four-year-old woman who hovered at death's door for days, before the medical team was able to pull her through.

The flu wasn't to be taken lightly, that's for sure.

A few minutes later, Ivan and Matt headed home. Kate disappeared into the staff lounge, but Dr. Drake Thorton didn't move.

There was a long moment of silence. When she couldn't stand it, she asked, "Something wrong, Dr. Thorton?"

"Huh?" He jerked his head up to meet her gaze as if he'd been deeply lost in his thoughts. "Nothing's wrong. Other than you should call me Drake the way everyone else does."

"I'll try to remember." She'd been careful not to be too friendly with the residents, mostly because they rotated in and out of Lifeline every three to four months. What was the point of getting chummy when she wasn't going to see them again?

Besides, she didn't have the time or the energy to foster new relationships. Her stomach rolled again, and she swallowed hard. "Excuse me." She rose from her seat and took her backpack into the small pilot's room adjacent to the lounge. Dropping down onto the cot, she opened the baggie of cheese and crackers and took a few small bites to help settle her queasy stomach.

She stared blindly at the wall for a moment, waiting for the cheese and crackers to do their magic. Unfortunately, her current condition wasn't the result of the flu. She closed her eyes and hung her head, struggling to remain calm.

Air Force Captain Calvin George had broken off their engagement, dumping her for another woman. Yet here she was in Milwaukee, flying the Lifeline chopper and pregnant with his child while he was serving their country overseas in Afghanistan with the new woman in his life, First Lieutenant Emily Forbes.

She'd sent him an email telling him about the baby but hadn't heard back. No doubt, he was either unable to get to a computer or he was planning to ignore the whole thing.

Fine. Whatever. She was a big girl and should have known better. They'd been engaged for just a few months when Cal had returned home on leave. It was only after they'd spent the week together that he'd told her he'd found someone else. The jerk didn't even have the guts to tell her up front. The knowledge that she'd spent an intimate week with him still burned.

Which is how she ended up like this. Pregnant. Single. Alone.

Responsibility weighed heavily on her shoulders. She absolutely needed to provide for her baby, but how long would she be allowed to fly? Certainly not past six or seven months along, that was for sure.

Did they make pregnancy flight suits? Doubtful.

Panic threatened to overwhelm her, but she shoved it aside, refusing to give in to the feeling of hopelessness. So what if she was in the journey of motherhood alone? She had some money saved from her own time in the Air Force.

It would be tight, depending on how long she'd be allowed to work in her current condition, but she and the baby would survive.

And thrive, she silently promised. No one would love this child more than she would.

Certainly not Captain Calvin George.

The main problem at the moment was that she still hadn't been in to see her OB. The appointment wasn't until after Christmas, and she'd been hoping to wait until she talked to her doctor about what her recommendation might be related to her ability to fly before telling Jared O'Connor, the medical director of Lifeline, about her condition.

As lousy as she was feeling, she feared her secret wouldn't be kept for long. Even Reese had picked up on how she looked pale and tired.

Apparently, that's what happened when you spent more time throwing up than eating. And when steep exhaustion was your constant companion.

The cheese and crackers helped settle her stomach, which was a good thing because her pager went off. Glancing at the screen, she noticed there was a call for an ICU to ICU transfer from a Racine hospital just twenty minutes away by air.

She brushed cracker crumbs from her flight suit and hurried out to where the chopper was located within the hangar. They kept it indoors during the winter months to minimize the threat of ice forming on the blades. Crouching down, she pulled the trolley holding the chopper in place until the bird was sitting out on the open landing pad.

Despite the sense of urgency radiating from Dr. Thorton and Kate, Megan took the time to go through the entire preflight checklist. Reese was a great pilot, one of her favorites here at Lifeline, but it had been drilled in her to always go through it again on your own. Better than depending on others when your safety and that of the entire crew was on the line.

Guilt stabbed deep. This was something she probably should have done before eating cheese and crackers.

She pulled on her helmet. "We're ready to go," she said, glancing at Dr. Thorton and Kate.

"Sounds good." Drake opened the chopper door for Kate, while she jumped into the pilot's seat. After settling in behind the stick, she connected with the paramedic base. "Base, this is Lifeline. Appears the FAA has cleared our route. We are ready to take off, over."

"Ten-four, Lifeline."

Megan revved the chopper's engine and did another quick check of her instrument panel before lifting the bird off the landing pad. She banked to the left, heading toward the Racine hospital where a critical care doctor was patiently waiting for them to arrive.

The motion of the chopper caused her stomach to dip and roll. She swallowed hard and did her best to ignore the urge to throw up.

No way was she going to let down the Lifeline crew. Or the patient depending on them to transport them to Trinity Medical Center.

Her stomach would just have to get over it.

DRAKE COULDN'T HELP BEING DRAWN to Megan's sweet husky voice through the intercom in his helmet. He'd been intrigued by the melodic tone the first time he'd flown with her and was irritated that he'd noticed.

His wife, Serena, and their unborn baby boy, Lance,

were dead. Gone forever. Barely a year ago, a couple of days before Christmas. He wasn't interested in Megan, or anyone for that matter.

He preferred being alone.

So this weird awareness of the pretty blonde pilot with the clear gray eyes needed to stop right now.

"Are you going to ask for an update on our patient's condition?" Kate's question pulled him from his thoughts.

"Yes." He cued the mic and asked the paramedic base to put him in touch with the provider at Racine. It took a moment for the doctor to come on the line. "This is Drake Thorton from Lifeline, I'm interested to hear how Betsy Jones, our thirty-nine-year-old septic patient, is doing."

"Hanging in there, but the flu has done a number on her kidneys. She has Addison's Disease and was severely dehydrated when she arrived and is now in full-blown kidney failure. We've been giving fluids necessary for combating her sepsis, but her urinary output isn't good. She may need continuous veno-venous filtration."

He knew that CVVH was used in cases where a patient wasn't stable enough to tolerate regular dialysis. It was a treatment that was only performed in an ICU setting because of the need to monitor the patient very closely. "Okay, thanks. If anything changes, please let me know." Drake disconnected from the call.

"I'm sure she'll be fine." Kate was the most cheerful woman he'd ever known, and he privately found her exhausting. Not that he begrudged her upbeat nature, but as he approached the anniversary of his wife and son's death, he could hardly stand her never-ending holiday spirit.

Yeah, just call him the Grinch. That's exactly how he felt about Christmas. It was one of the reasons he'd offered to work twelve-hour shifts on both Christmas Eve and Christmas Day. Anything to help keep him busy.

Hopefully, Kate would be spending time with her husband rather than working. As far as he was concerned, all the happily married and recently engaged staff could be off the holiday. He'd rather not hear about wedding plans, upcoming pregnancy news, etc.

He'd had all that once.

But not anymore.

He stared out the window, watching the skies for the possibility of bird strikes. He'd been taught it was a potential threat to bringing down a chopper. Although, he didn't think Lifeline had ever experienced such a phenomenon. Or if they had, he hadn't heard about it.

"ETA ten minutes." Megan's sweet voice filtered into his thoughts.

"Roger that." He glanced at Kate who was watching him thoughtfully. He'd heard through the rumor mill that she'd charmed her husband by being relentlessly cheerful and upbeat, and he hoped she didn't think he needed the same sort of treatment.

"Cheer up, Drake. Where there is life, there is hope."

He wanted to groan but lifted a brow instead. "Thanks for the advice, although I don't know why you think I need to cheer up. I'm fine."

Kate's smile held a note of sadness. "You can't fool a pro like me."

He decided to let it go. "Megan, do you have an update on the time frame of our arrival?"

"ETA less than five minutes." Even as Megan spoke, the chopper banked to the right, no doubt heading for the hospital's rooftop landing pad. Most hospitals had them placed on the roof, although he'd been to several smaller hospitals who had them on the ground level.

He was anxious to get to work. Anything to avoid additional conversation with Kate Weber.

They landed with a barely felt thud. He pushed open the door and jumped down. He moved around back to pull out the gurney. Kate quickly joined him, and together they headed inside. Away from the chopper, they stripped off their helmets and stashed them beneath the gurney.

Kate knew the way to the ICU, which was good as he'd only been here once before and couldn't remember.

"The Lifeline crew is here," someone called out as they entered the critical care unit. It was easy to tell which patient they were looking for—the bedside straight ahead was surrounded by several hospital staff.

"Dr. Thorton?" A tall man with salt-and-pepper hair stepped toward him. "I'm Rich Gillis, we spoke earlier on the phone."

"Hi." Drake shook the guy's hand. "Any change in Betsy's condition?"

Rich grimaced. "We just started her on a vasopressor to keep her mean arterial blood pressure above sixty. But it's at a low dose, hopefully it won't be a problem during transport."

Drake nodded, although the news was a bit concerning. Once they accepted the transfer, the patient was their responsibility. But he also knew if they didn't get her to Trinity Medical Center, she might die. "How are her labs?"

Kate worked on getting their equipment connected as he familiarized himself with the latest lab values and vital signs. When he was satisfied they had what they needed, he helped with the equipment.

"Ready?" He glanced at Kate, who nodded.

They wheeled the patient out of the ICU and onto the elevator that would take them up to the helipad where Megan had the chopper waiting.

He donned his helmet before pushing the gurney out into the cold December air. In these conditions, the helmet provided warmth as well as protection. At six feet two inches tall, he always wanted to crouch down to make sure he wasn't hit by the whirling chopper blades.

He and Kate lifted Becky and the gurney into the back hatch. He held the gurney firm as Kate jumped inside to pull her the rest of the way inside. By the time he joined Kate, she was already documenting the first set of vital signs.

Becky's blood pressure started to dip. Kate had placed the headphones on Becky's head, even though their young patient was intubated and on a ventilator with a low dose sedative running.

"Becky, squeeze my hand if you can hear me," Kate said.

Their patient didn't respond.

"That's okay, I know you can still hear me. We're on our way to Trinity Medical Center, where the experts are going to take good care of you." Kate glanced at him, then switched the microphone so their patient couldn't overhear. "I don't like the way her blood pressure is dropping."

"Me either. Go up on the epinephrine."

Kate did as instructed, but instead of going up, their patient's blood pressure dropped lower.

Something was wrong. He tried not to panic. "I need to look at her central line." Drake knew that if her central line had become dislodged, the medication wouldn't be in her blood vessels where it belonged. The idea of placing a new central line while in the air was intimidating, but he'd done it once before.

If needed, he could do it again.

Peering at the insertion site, he could see the catheter was out farther than it had been and the area around it damp from where the epinephrine was leaking. "Get me a new central line."

Kate opened the equipment as he prepared the opposite side of Becky's chest with antimicrobial solution and donned sterile gloves. His heart was hammering so loudly he feared Kate and Megan could hear it.

"Dr. Thorton, would you like me to divert to a closer hospital?" Megan asked.

"No, but that might change if this doesn't work." He found Megan's voice soothing, although he was irked by her continued use of his formal title. Pushing that aside, he concentrated on inserting the needle into Becky's subclavian vein.

He wasn't sure how, maybe God was helping from above, but he hit the vein and easily threaded the catheter. When he had it in place, he held it steady so Kate could connect the IV tubing connected to the epinephrine drip. In seconds, Becky's blood pressure responded to the medication in her bloodstream.

Blowing out a silent sigh of relief, he secured the line and covered it with an occlusive dressing. "We're good, Megan. We should make it to Trinity without a problem."

"I'm glad," Megan responded.

The rest of the trip was uneventful. They arrived at Trinity Medical Center and handed Becky's care off to the medical intensive care team. Back in the chopper, he listened as Megan spoke to the base about their plan to return to Lifeline.

"Nice work, Doc." Kate grinned. "You were steady as a rock."

"Thanks." He hadn't felt steady as a rock but was glad

the line had been placed in the correct spot without an issue. When they landed at Lifeline, Kate jumped out first, and he climbed down after her, moving more slowly.

"Excuse me." Megan practically ran past him in her haste to get inside the hangar, ripping off her helmet as she went. He frowned and quickened his pace to catch up. When he went inside the debriefing room, he heard her throwing up in the bathroom.

"Megan?" He rapped lightly on the door. "Are you okay?"

"Go away." Her voice was muffled.

Did she have the flu? The Lifeline crew hadn't been impacted by the virus so far, and they had all received their required flu vaccine, but he knew several of the ED staff had been sick over the past few weeks.

He stayed where he was, waiting for her to emerge. When she came out of the bathroom, she actually looked better, her eyes bright and her cheeks rosy, as if throwing up had helped.

For a moment he was puzzled, then it hit him. Serena had been the exact same way. "You're pregnant."

She sucked in a harsh breath, staring at him in horror. Then she brushed past him and disappeared into the pilot's room.

2

You're pregnant.

The accusatory words echoed over and over in Megan's mind as she sought the sanctuary of the pilot's room. It was the only place in the entire hangar that provided the Lifeline pilots a bit of privacy.

Until now. Drake slapped his hand on the door, preventing her from closing it behind her. She turned to face him, lifting her chin. "Leave me alone, Drake."

For a moment his gaze flickered, and she realized she'd called him by his first name. *Idiot.*

"You are, aren't you?" His dark brown eyes stared relentlessly into hers.

Megan knew this could go one of two ways. She could try to convince him she wasn't pregnant, despite the way she'd just tossed her breakfast, or she could tell him the truth and find a way to convince him to keep the news a secret for a while.

If he didn't believe her, he might tell Jared anyway, so best try to convince him to keep quiet.

"Please, come in and sit down." She stepped back so he could join her in the small room.

He dropped into the only chair while she set her helmet aside and perched on the edge of the bed. For a long moment neither of them said anything.

Where to start?

"Are you supposed to be flying in your condition?"

She stifled a sigh. "I'm a little over three months along, so yes, I'm able to fly. I haven't even had my first doctor's appointment yet, which is the only reason I haven't told Jared. And I respectfully ask you to keep this news to yourself. I don't want Jared to hear this news through the rumor mill. I will talk to him after I see the doctor."

Drake's gaze dropped momentarily to her ringless hand, before shifting away. "You have to take better care of yourself or your secret won't be safe for long."

She bristled. "I am taking care of myself. It's not my fault that food isn't sitting well with me. As a doctor, you should understand the symptoms of pregnancy. I'm doing the best I can while being in a difficult situation."

"Maybe you should take a leave of absence until you're feeling better."

"Not interested." She was fast losing her patience with him. "This isn't really any of your business, Dr. Thorton, but I would appreciate some privacy about my personal life. As I said, I don't want to be the subject of the rumor mill. Women have babies all the time; it's perfectly natural. I don't need advice or help."

"Not even from the baby's father?"

She flushed. "Cal is in Afghanistan and in a relationship with another woman. So yes, not even from the baby's father. I don't need his help, or anyone else's."

Drake winced and let out a heavy sigh. "Listen, Megan, I feel for you." He hesitated, then added, "Are you going to keep it?"

"What?" She stared at him in shock. "Yes. Again, not that it's any of your business."

"Sorry." His expression was chagrined. "I shouldn't have asked. But I am curious about what you're going to do if you get sick while flying."

"I won't. And if I do, I'll deal with it." She didn't appreciate being interrogated, yet she knew Drake was only saying the same things Jared would. Except the part about asking if she planned to keep the baby. That was just weird. But the rest was exactly what Jared would want to know.

The difference being that Jared had the ability to ground her.

Permanently.

"When is your OB appointment?"

"The Monday after Christmas, which is only a little over two weeks away." She stared at him for a long moment. "Well? Are you going to tell him? Or give me the chance to talk to my doctor first?"

Drake hesitated so long she thought she'd lost the battle, but then he reluctantly nodded. "I'll hold off, as long as you make me a promise."

She eyed him warily. "What kind of promise?"

"That you won't do anything to put the crew at risk."

A flash of anger hit hard. "Of course I won't! What kind of pilot do you think I am? I've been flying choppers since I was twenty-two years old in the Air Force. I would never put anyone flying with me in danger."

He looked surprised at the news and nodded. "Glad to hear it. I didn't realize you were in the Air Force."

She hadn't meant to talk about herself, so how was it that she'd not only blabbed about how Cal was in Afghanistan and seeing someone else, but she'd blurted out the details of her military background?

She must be losing it.

"Yes, well, I was. Now if you'll excuse me, I'm going to try to eat breakfast again."

Drake stared at her for a long moment before rising to his feet. "All right, I'll give you some privacy."

Relief made her feel light-headed. Or maybe it was the lack of food. Either way, she stayed seated just in case. The last thing she wanted to do was to fall flat on her face in front of him. "Thank you."

Drake made his way to the door. He paused, glancing back at her over his shoulder. "I'm sorry I pried into your personal life. It's just—I was adopted. So I was curious."

Really? Very interesting. "That's okay. I didn't realize you were adopted."

He shrugged but chose not to say anything more on that subject. "You know, he's a fool."

She blinked. "Who?"

"Cal." Without saying anything more, Drake left the pilot's room.

Nibbling again on cheese and crackers, she found herself smiling. Because Drake was right.

Cal was a fool. She glanced down at her still-flat abdomen and placed her hand over her stomach.

"Don't worry. I promise we're going to be just fine without him."

From now on, providing for her baby was her only priority.

❧

DRAKE JOINED Kate in the lounge where she was FaceTiming with her husband and daughter. "I know, I miss you too, Carly. But I'm off the weekend and so is Daddy, so we'll do something fun then, okay?"

Averting his gaze from the mushy domestic scene, he thought about what Megan had revealed.

He couldn't believe he'd asked her if she intended to keep the baby. What was wrong with him? Megan's decisions weren't any of his business. He was lucky she hadn't smacked him for asking such a personal question. Yet he couldn't help wondering why it was that God had taken his wife and son while providing Megan an unplanned baby.

Not that she didn't deserve to be happy, she did. He had no doubt Megan would be a great mother, but for whatever reason, he kept thinking about what Serena had gone through during her pregnancy. Not just the morning sickness and, frankly, all-day sickness, but the fatigue and mood swings. The way Serena had leaned on him for support.

How would Megan manage everything alone? Being a single mother wasn't easy. It was, in fact, the reason many women went the adoption route.

Why did he care? This wasn't his problem.

Yet he couldn't seem to get Megan's plight out of his mind.

Was he doing the right thing by holding off telling Jared? It wasn't his responsibility to let their boss know, but he hoped keeping quiet didn't come back to bite him. Megan had looked better after throwing up, so he was certain she'd be fine moving forward.

Kate finally finished her phone call, coming over to sit beside him on the sofa. "Interested in playing cards? I play a mean game of gin rummy."

"Not really." He wasn't much for cards and would have preferred to be left alone. But he felt certain Kate wouldn't take no for an answer. "Excuse me, I have some education to get caught up on." He gestured toward the computer sitting on a small table in the corner, then stood and crossed over to sit down in front of the monitor.

Since he did have an outstanding education module to complete, he logged in. He took his time, more so to avoid more small talk with Kate or to be sucked into playing a game.

After he finished his educational requirement, he checked his personal email. There was a message there from an unknown woman, the email originating from the adoption site called Find Your Family he'd signed up for well over a year ago.

He swallowed hard. At the time, he'd thought searching for his birth mother was the right thing to do. After all, he and Serena were having a baby. He knew very little about his mother's medical background and nothing at all about his father. Not to mention, what if anything may have changed in the past twenty-eight years since he'd been born?

But now, he wasn't so sure he wanted to know. He was staring at the screen without clicking to open the message when his pager went off. He instantly shut down the program and logged off the computer as Kate read the details of their next call out loud.

"Neonatal transfer from Sheboygan to Children's Memorial Hospital." Kate glanced at Drake warily. "You're trained to take care of kiddos, right?"

"Yes, I'm cross-trained in pediatrics." He didn't add that he hadn't done much peds since losing his wife and son. "What about you?"

"Of course. That was one of the first things Jared did when he took over, make sure everyone was cross-trained in peds." Kate crossed over to grab the duffel bag of supplies. "We'll need to take our portable isolette, in place of the gurney."

The portable isolette was stored off to the side covered in plastic, ready to go. It was just like the isolette they used in the hospital, mounted on a cart with wheels. He went over, pulled off the plastic covering, and pushed it through the debriefing room on their way out to the hangar. The chopper was sitting where they'd left it, and Megan was already climbing into the cockpit.

Drake pulled his gaze from her, focusing instead on the job he needed to do. He and Kate removed the gurney and lifted the portable isolette into the hatch in its place. When they were seated in the chopper, he listened to Megan's smooth husky voice and couldn't help picturing how pretty she looked with her blond hair pulled back and pink color in her cheeks.

"Base, this is Lifeline requesting permission to take off." Megan's voice was calm and steady.

"Roger, Lifeline, you've been cleared to go."

"Ten-four."

Within moments they were airborne, banking to the right as Megan flew them north toward Sheboygan. Pushing his curiosity over the email message aside, Drake focused on the transfer at hand. He waited until they'd steadied their pace before making the call to the labor and delivery unit at Sheboygan.

"This is Dr. Thorton, I'm calling from Lifeline requesting an update on Infant Male Browning."

"I'm Dr. Roche," a female voice said. "The baby is thirty-two weeks old. He's been intubated and placed on a ventilator, but we are way in over our heads here. What is your estimated time of arrival?"

"Just a moment." Drake switched to the internal channel. "Megan? What's our ETA?"

"Thirteen minutes, maybe less."

"Thanks." Drake switched back to the all communication channel. "We're roughly thirteen minutes out. How are the infant's vital signs?"

"He's extremely tachy, and I'm not sure why." The female doctor's voice held a note of panic. "He's also very hypothermic. I'm afraid he's going to die."

"Focus on the basics," Drake said calmly. "Have you done a head scan? He doesn't have a brain injury, does he?"

"No brain injury."

"Good. Is it possible he's septic?"

"Maybe, let me see if he's gotten his antibiotic. Darcy? Have you infused his antibiotic yet? Well, get on it." Dr. Roche sighed, then added, "The antibiotic is being given right now."

"Keep him warm, calm, and hydrated. We'll be there soon."

"Thanks." Dr. Roche disconnected from the call.

"Sounds serious," Megan said, her husky voice sending a shiver of awareness through him. Get a grip, he reminded himself.

He locked eyes for a moment with Kate, before responding in what he hoped was a casual tone. "Yes, but you'd be surprised. Babies are stronger than they look."

Kate lifted a brow as if amazed that he was trying to put their pilot at ease. He looked away, trying not to think of how innocent and still his son had looked after the car accident his wife had been in.

His wife had died of a massive head injury and his son,

Lance, had been stillborn as a result of the crash. None of the neonatal team's resuscitative efforts had worked to bring him back.

He'd lost them both that day, not quite a year ago. He found himself hoping and praying he wouldn't lose Infant Male Browning either.

The time seemed to drag by, but soon Megan said, "ETA three minutes."

He took a deep breath and tried to settle his racing heart. Being cross-trained in peds was one thing, taking care of a critically ill preemie was something completely different.

Megan banked the chopper to the left as they approached the rooftop landing pad. She set the chopper down so gently he didn't even feel the bump.

"Let's go." He pushed open the door and jumped down. Kate followed, helping him pull the isolette out of the hatch.

Kate hurried ahead, again more familiar with the hospital layout than he was. She led the way into the labor and delivery area, where they were then directed to the correct room.

Drake pushed the isolette into the room and turned his attention to the baby. The infant was tiny, barely four pounds, and the endotracheal tube coming out of his mouth looked too large compared to the rest of his body. He had an IV threaded into a vein in his arm with the antibiotic medication infusing at a slow rate.

"Thank goodness you're here." A female physician wearing a nametag that read Allison Roche stepped away from the isolette. "His heart rate has come down a bit, hanging at one hundred seventy-five beats per minute rather than one ninety, but there hasn't been any other change for the better."

"Are you warming him?" He checked the mattress beneath the baby, glad to feel it was warm.

"Yes, but his temperature is still subnormal." Dr. Roche looked as if she might cry. "I can't believe this. I tried to stop the mother's contractions long enough to transfer her to Trinity Medical Center, but he wasn't interested in staying put. I had no choice but to deliver."

"It's okay. We'll take it from here." He waited until Kate had the heart monitor switched over before lifting the preemie with two hands and placing him on their isolette.

The infant's arms and legs flailed a bit at the sudden movement, then he settled back down. They had the mattress pad already heated up to help keep him warm. Drake took a minute to double-check the ventilator settings before setting up their portable vent. Then he quickly disconnected the hospital vent and reconnected the little guy to their portable machine.

"It's okay, little man. We're going to take care of you." He hadn't realized he'd spoken out loud until Kate added, "Yes, we will."

He pulled himself together and cleared his throat. "Ready?"

"Of course." Between them, they pushed the isolette out of the labor and delivery unit and to the elevator leading up to the helipad.

Despite the keen sense of urgency, they didn't rush. Again, it seemed to take forever to get Infant Male Browning up to the landing pad and into the chopper.

Once they were seated with their helmets in place, he cued his mic. "We're all set," he told Megan.

"Base, this is Lifeline requesting clearance to head to Children's Memorial Hospital."

"Roger, Lifeline, you're clear to go."

Megan lifted the chopper up into the air. He kept his gaze on the baby's monitor, noting his heart rate was slowly coming down. It was now 170 and heading in the right direction.

"He's so little," Kate said. "It's amazing what modern medicine can do these days, isn't it?"

Drake bit back a sarcastic reply. All the modern medicine in the world hadn't saved his wife and son. But that wasn't the issue here.

Keeping Infant Male Browning alive was.

"Looks like his antibiotic is only a fourth of the way infused," Kate said, peering at the burette chamber used for neonatal infusions. "I'm going to double-check the rate."

Drake frowned, doing the math calculation in his head. The antibiotic should be further along by his estimation, based on the conversation he had with Dr. Roche as to when it was started.

He pushed his gloved hands through the opening of the isolette and gently palpated the little guy's IV site. His gut clenched when he realized the vein had been blown.

"Stop the drip." He glanced at Kate. "We need a new IV."

He thought he heard Megan draw a quick breath but concentrated on searching for another potential vein. All he could see was a scalp vein on the left side, the one closest to him.

"I need a twenty-six gauge butterfly IV."

Kate poked through their duffle of supplies until she found what he needed.

Drake gently washed the area on the little guy's scalp with antimicrobial solution, then took a deep breath and threaded the slender needle into the tiny vein. There was a flash of blood, indicating he was in the right spot, but he didn't relax.

Don't blow, don't blow, he mentally urged as he secured the IV in place and then connected the tubing. At his nod, Kate opened the IV fluids, making sure the rate was the same as it had been before.

"His heart rate is back up to 180," Kate said.

"Is everything okay?" Megan's voice held an underlying note of anxiety. "Do you need me to divert the chopper to another hospital?"

"No, stay on course. The sooner we get to Children's Memorial, the better."

"All right. I'm going to fly at a higher elevation so we can increase our speed."

"Sounds good." He strove to sound confident when he was anything but.

This little baby was depending on him to keep him safe. The way he hadn't kept his son, Lance, safe. Granted, he wasn't in the car when the accident had happened, but he should have been.

If he had, maybe he would have died too. There were days he wished he had. Living without his wife and son had been the most difficult thing for him to do.

But right now, he understood that this was a chance to save someone else, like this little boy.

If he was able.

"Heart rate at one seventy-six," Kate said, interrupting his thoughts. "His temperature is closer to normal."

It wasn't much better. Had he been wrong about the IV? No, feeling the infant's arm, he could tell the dressing was damp from where the fluid had escaped. Infant IVs were known not to last very long, twenty-four hours at the most, sometimes less.

Logically he knew it would take time for the antibiotic to circulate through his system.

Drake swallowed hard, battling a wave of helplessness. At this point, miles in the air, there wasn't anything more they could do.

Except watch, wait, and pray.

3

_____

The underlying note of fear and worry in Drake's voice had Megan wishing there was more she could do to help. Thankfully, her earlier nausea had eased to a tolerable level, so she could concentrate on flying.

With a sure hand on the stick, she increased their altitude to take advantage of the tailwind. By her calculation, the move would shave five minutes off their flight time.

It sounded as if Drake and Kate needed every one of those minutes.

"Base, this is Lifeline." Drake's voice was steady, but she could tell he was still concerned. "I'd like to speak with the accepting physician at Children's Memorial. The NICU team needs to meet us on the helipad when we land."

"Ten-four, Lifeline. We'll get back to you."

Megan swept her gaze over the sunny skies, glad there was no threat of snow or freezing rain to slow them down. This time of year the risk of bird strikes was less than in the spring, when all the various breeds of geese returned from wintering in the south. Still, it was always better to be on alert as it was not unheard of to have a duck or a goose break through the windshield of a helicopter.

"Lifeline, this is the paramedic base. We have Dr. Nunzio from the neonatal ICU on the line for Dr. Thorton."

"This is Dr. Thorton, and I have a preemie up here that is still severely tachycardic despite the antibiotic that is infusing. I'm afraid he's showing signs of sepsis. Requesting a hot unload."

"Have you checked the IV site?" Nunzio asked.

"Yes. New IV has been placed in a scalp vein."

Megan winced at the image of an IV catheter going into a tiny infant's scalp. Her stomach rolled, but she ignored it. This was why she was a pilot and not a member of the medical team.

Her admiration for Drake annoyed her. He was a doctor, just like all the others she'd watched come and go. No reason to believe he was special. Nosy? Yes. Special? No.

"Okay, we'll meet you on the helipad. What's your ETA?" Nunzio asked.

"Megan?"

She cleared her throat and cued her mic. "ETA roughly eight minutes."

"We'll see you soon, then." Nunzio disconnected from the line.

"You're making good time, Megan. Thanks." Drake's warm gratitude made her flush. Good thing he was in the back of the chopper where he couldn't see her.

Listening to his deep voice in her ear was hard enough.

"We have a decent tailwind putting more air under our belly."

Drake made a sound that almost sounded like a rusty laugh. "Good to know. I appreciate the extra lift."

She found herself smiling in response as she guided the

chopper through the air following the established flight pattern. Choppers generally flew at much lower altitudes than jet airplanes, but there were enough small prop planes owned by amateur pilots—not to mention an increased use of personal drones, which could create havoc if there was a deviation from the flight plan.

After three minutes, she brought the chopper lower to begin their descent to Children's Memorial located near Trinity Medical Center. Out the corner of her eye, she saw a mallard duck flying dangerously close. She eased the stick to the right in an effort to avoid it. Thankfully, the bird disappeared from view without a problem.

"ETA less than three minutes," she said through the intercom.

"Good." Drake sounded relieved. "This little guy is hanging in there, but I'll be glad to hand him over to the NICU team."

She could understand where he was coming from. Focusing her attention on the landing before her, she brought the bird gently down onto the landing pad. She kept the blades whirling as Drake and Kate jumped down, transporting their tiny patient to the team of medical staff waiting for them near the doorway.

She could see the entire team crowded around the small isolette for a long moment before they disappeared inside the hospital. Megan rotated her shoulders in an attempt to ease her stress. She loved flying and appreciated being able to do a job she enjoyed that also helped people. But listening as patients decompensated wasn't easy. She tended to take their patient's poor condition personally.

Which was crazy since she was just the pilot. Not the doctor, nurse, or paramedic in charge.

Drake and Kate returned five minutes later, stashing the

now empty isolette into the back hatch, then ducking beneath the rotating blades and climbing aboard. She cued her mic. "Everything go okay?"

"Yeah. The little guy is in good hands." Drake sounded almost cheerful. "Thanks for getting us here so quickly."

"Of course." It was her job, but she understood that some pilots weren't as responsive to the needs of the care team. "I'd like to refuel before we head back to Trinity Medical Center."

"Sure thing."

Megan discussed the need to refuel with the paramedic base and made the necessary stop at the closest airfield. The Lifeline hangar had fuel, but they tried to use that only in an emergency or as needed for an extra-long flight.

The stop didn't take long, and fifteen minutes later, she landed the bird at the Lifeline hangar. Her stomach was beginning to sour again, and a glance at her watch indicated it was closer to lunchtime than she'd realized. Following Drake and Kate into the hangar, she ducked into the pilot's room to find her last cheese square and saltine cracker. She debated eating it or saving the snack for later. After all, it was nearly lunchtime. She decided to hold off.

When she emerged, Drake was sitting in the debriefing room as if waiting for her. She hesitated, then crossed over toward him. "Something wrong?"

"No, just thought it might be nice to grab a bite to eat at the deli across the street." He shrugged. "It won't take long, and we can always head back if a call comes in."

"Oh, sure. I was just thinking of getting some lunch." Megan tried to sound casual even though her heart jumped a bit.

He slowly stood, towering over her five-foot-five-inch frame. "Kate brought her lunch, so it's just you and me."

Really? She hesitated, then realized she'd look like an idiot if she backed out. Besides, she was hungry and hadn't brought anything but the cheese and crackers to eat. She forced a smile. "Great, let's go."

She drew on her navy blue Lifeline jacket as Drake did the same. He held the door open for her, the way her father always had for her mother.

The way Cal never had.

Whatever. She told herself that making these sorts of comparisons wasn't healthy. There were plenty of men who were better and worse than Cal. And it didn't matter anyway since she was over him.

Well, mostly over him. The burn of resentment lingered. And the baby she carried was a constant reminder of the foolish mistake she'd made in trusting him.

A cold gust caught her hair, blowing it over her face. She tucked it behind her ears, thinking it may have been smart to wear a hat. "Brr. I hope the wind coming in from the north isn't going to pick up speed. I'll have to check the radar, make sure there isn't a storm brewing."

"I hope not." As Drake walked beside her, their fingers brushed lightly, sending a strange tingle of awareness shooting through her. "Although I'd be happy if we didn't have to do any more pediatric transfers. That last one was rough."

She eyed him curiously. "You handled it well. And the baby is in a much better place, right? If we weren't there to transport him, what was his chance of surviving?"

Drake grimaced. "Slim, for sure. Okay, I'm glad we were there for the little guy. I hope he does well."

"He will." Megan decided it was best to think positively. "You should put him on your list of patients to follow up on."

A crooked smile tugged at the corner of Drake's mouth. "Already did that. But I'm off tomorrow, so it will have to be on Saturday."

She was off the following day, too, but decided not to mention it. This weird awareness between them was distracting enough. The last thing she wanted was to sound as if she were hinting around to see him the following day.

Not that he'd be interested in her that way regardless. He'd looked pretty intense when she'd admitted to being pregnant. Especially when he'd asked if she planned on keeping the baby.

It made her curious about the circumstances around his adoption.

The deli parking lot wasn't too crowded, maybe because they'd arrived at eleven thirty, before the noon rush. Drake leaned around her to open the door. The same time she stepped forward, a young couple came out, causing her to step back. She bumped into Drake, his arms coming around to steady her against him. A hint of his musky scent swirled around her and the shimmering awareness intensified.

Must be the hormones. She tried to shake it off, hoping Drake wouldn't pick up on the tension. Yeah, it had to be her hormones, they were all over the place because of her pregnancy.

The couple barely acknowledged them, brushing past them as if in a hurry to get somewhere.

"Are you okay?" Drake's deep voice rumbled near her ear.

"Yes, fine." Her voice sounded breathy, and she quickly stepped over the threshold. The deli was decorated for Christmas, with loops of garland hanging above the cashiers and a tiny Christmas tree decorated with bright lights and festively wrapped gifts, likely fake ones, underneath. "So pretty. I love the Christmas decorations."

Drake didn't respond, his gaze centered on the menu on the side wall as if she hadn't spoken. This was the second time he avoided talking about the Christmas holiday, the first being when Ivan brought up the impact of his daughter behaving better under the watchful eye of Eddie the Elf, and she didn't think it was a coincidence.

Related to his adoption? Or something else? Regardless, Drake's problems weren't any of her business. He had a right to his privacy, the same way she did. Just because he'd pried into her personal life, she didn't have to do the same.

No matter how much she wanted to.

Perusing the menu, she was glad to see there were lots of options. In the end, she decided on a grilled cheese and tomato soup. Plain fare, maybe, but it was the only thing that appealed to her finicky stomach.

"Ready to order?" Drake glanced at her.

"Sure." She moved up to the open cashier and requested the grilled cheese and tomato soup. When she reached into her pocket to pay, Drake put a hand on her arm.

"My treat." He gently nudged her aside. "I'll have the French dip sandwich."

Megan shot him an exasperated glance. "I can afford to buy my own lunch."

"I know." Drake shrugged off her annoyance. "My treat. You were a big help on that transport back from Sheboygan."

"I didn't do anything special. Flying is my job, Drake. Just like saving lives is yours."

He nodded and took their number to an empty table. "Yes, but you're always so in tune as to what's going on with our patients."

His compliment made her blush, and she averted her gaze. "Well, thanks. But buying me lunch isn't necessary."

He didn't say anything more, and a few minutes later, a runner came out with their respective meals.

As they ate, she found herself wondering if Drake would have offered to buy if Kate had been with them?

Somehow, she didn't think so. And she wasn't sure what to make of that.

DRAKE MENTALLY CALLED himself all kinds of an idiot to have bought Megan's lunch as if this was some sort of date.

It wasn't.

He didn't date. Ever.

What was he thinking? More than once he'd found himself mesmerized by Megan's light gray eyes, the way they'd lit up when she'd noticed the Christmas decorations.

What would she think if she saw his bare-bones apartment? No personal photos, except the ones of his wife, pregnant with their son, hiding in the bottom drawer of his dresser.

And definitely no Christmas decorations.

The unread email from the Find Your Family website in his inbox haunted him. He wanted to read it almost as much as he wanted to delete it.

"Hmm. This hits the spot." Megan beamed at him from across the table.

The corner of his mouth quirked up in a smile. "Glad your stomach has settled down."

"Me too."

They ate in silence for several minutes. He pushed his personal issues aside. He could deal with the stupid email later. Business inside the deli picked up, to the point there were long lines almost out the door.

Megan lifted her head. "Did you hear that?"

He glanced around in confusion. "What?"

"The wind. It's getting worse." She pulled her cell phone from her pocket. "I'm worried we're going to end up being grounded for the rest of our shift."

"I hope not." He really, really hoped not. Kate was nice enough, but spending hours with her begging him to play cards would be exhausting. "Maybe it sounds worse than it is?"

"Maybe." She stared at the weather app on her phone. It was more sophisticated than the basic one he used. "Looks like the wind is still coming in from the north but picking up speed. Wind gusts of thirty-five miles per hour are expected to continue for the next couple of hours."

"And that means—what? We can't fly?"

She grimaced and set the phone on the table beside her. "We generally can fly in winds up to forty miles per hour, but there's obviously more risk. Plus we can't go at higher speeds like we did earlier to get that little baby to Children's Memorial."

He nodded, relaxing a bit. "Okay, that makes sense, but even if we can't go as fast because of the wind, it doesn't mean we shouldn't transport patients. Often coming to a level one trauma center like Trinity is the best option they have to survive."

She hesitated, then shrugged. "You're right, but we might have to prioritize. A transfer that could be done via ground transport may have to be denied."

He wanted to argue, but he knew her logic made sense. This wouldn't be the first time or the last, they'd often had to make patients wait over the past few months that he'd been flying with the Lifeline team. "Yeah, okay. We'll prioritize so we're only responding to trauma calls and urgent or emergent transfers."

Megan nodded. "Sounds like a plan, then."

He thought about Infant Male Browning, one of the more emergent transfers he'd participated in so far. If they hadn't been able to fly—he suppressed a shudder.

Deep down, he felt certain the preemie wouldn't have made it longer than a day or two at the most if they hadn't transferred him to Children's Memorial.

His sandwich congealed in his gut, and he took a deep breath and let it out slowly. Maybe there wouldn't be very many pediatric calls coming in.

The only thing worse would be an OB trauma call.

"Are you finished?" Megan's voice interrupted his depressing thoughts.

"Yeah, I'm good."

"Me too. We'd better head back." Megan had finished her soup and half her grilled cheese sandwich. He noticed she wrapped the other half to take back to Lifeline. She stood and gathered their garbage together.

He followed her as she threaded her way through the crowd, pausing long enough to drop their trash into the garbage before heading for the door. He wasn't entirely sure what happened next, other than Megan tripped and fell, hitting the ground with a hard thud.

"Megan!" Panic seized his throat as he pushed past the customers to reach her side. She was sprawled on her abdomen, but she was trying to push herself up to her hands and knees. He gently held her in place. "Just stay where you are for a moment, okay?"

She relaxed beneath his touch. He glanced around in annoyance at the customers who barely made room for them. "Back up," he said in an authoritative tone. "I'm a doctor."

Surprisingly, the crowd did as he asked, moving out of the way to give them room. A woman picked up the to-go bag she'd dropped. He calmed his heart. "Where do you hurt?"

She hesitated. "Mostly my hands and knees."

"Okay, here, let me help you up."

She didn't argue when he put his hands beneath her arms to help lever her upright. She let out a low moan but managed to stand on her own two feet.

"Are you sure you're all right?"

"Yes." Her cheeks were red with embarrassment as she brushed dirt from the knees of her flight suit. "I'm fine."

"What happened?"

She shook her head, took her to-go bag, then moved toward the door. He wanted to protest but decided she wouldn't listen anyway, so he quickly caught up to her outside.

"Megan." He lightly grasped her arm. "Seriously, stop for a minute. Are you sure you aren't hurt?"

"You mean other than my pride?" She glanced down at the dark spots on her knees. "Bruised, that's all."

"What happened?"

She grimaced. "I'm a klutz. I managed to trip over some-one's feet."

"I can't believe no one tried to help you up." He raked his gaze over her, needing the reassurance that she was in fact okay. "No abdominal cramps or anything?"

She blushed again and looked away. "No. I told you I'm fine. Let's go."

The tightness across his chest eased as he realized she'd

be fine. He willed his heart rate to return to normal as they walked back over to the Lifeline hangar.

It occurred to him that, despite his efforts to remain aloof from the people he worked with on this temporary assignment, Megan Hoffman was getting to him in a way no other woman had in the year his wife had been gone.

And he didn't like it one bit.

4

Ignoring the lingering pain in her hands and knees was much easier than ignoring the impact of Drake's strong hands helping her off the deli floor. She'd never been so flustered by a man in her life.

And she wasn't thrilled about experiencing it now.

First he overhears her throwing up in the bathroom and confronts her with being pregnant, then he has to pick her up off the floor of the deli. Why couldn't she come across as a confident, competent pilot around him rather than a needy, klutzy pregnant woman?

Shaking her head at her foolishness, she followed Drake and Kate into the Lifeline hangar. Instead of following them into the lounge, she ducked into the pilot's room to put her sandwich in the fridge, then came back to the debriefing room. She took a seat behind the radar screen so she could evaluate the weather. The winds were staying in the thirty-five miles per hour range, but she knew that could easily change without warning.

Focusing on their current flying conditions assisted in steadying her tumultuous emotions. It also helped that

Drake and Kate disappeared into the lounge. Twice within an hour, she caught herself resting her hand protectively on her lower abdomen. At this rate, she wondered how long her secret would be safe.

The way things were going? Not very.

Megan inwardly debated her next steps while watching the radar screen. After thirty minutes of hemming and hawing, she logged into her work email and sent a message to Jared, asking to meet with him at his earliest convenience for a nonurgent personal issue. After hitting the send button, she sat back in her seat, hoping Jared would be so busy with the upcoming holidays and his own growing family, seeing as Shelly had given birth to a baby girl a couple of months ago, that he wouldn't set up the meeting until after her doctor's appointment.

Which only proved to be wishful thinking as Jared replied that he'd be happy to talk to her on Tuesday, which was her next weekday to work since she was off on Friday and Monday but on the schedule for the weekend.

Tuesday. Only four days away.

Swallowing a sigh, she wrote back and agreed to meet with him on Tuesday, saying again it was nothing urgent. At least he hadn't called her directly to ask what was up.

Their next page came in about an hour later. Megan looked at the message on the screen, taking note that the call was for a semitruck vs car crash on the interstate. Patient was a fifty-two-year-old man with a traumatic chest injury.

No way to put off flying to a trauma call, but at least the crash scene was close, only a ten-minute ride from the hangar. By the time she'd pulled the chopper out of the hangar, Drake and Kate were ready to go.

Less than five minutes later, she had the helicopter in

the air, heading for the interstate. She stayed low because of the wind gusts, even though there was an increased risk of hitting power lines, drones, and birds when flying at lower altitudes.

The upside? It was easier to perform an emergency landing from a lower altitude.

Not that she wanted to prove it anytime in the near future.

When the crash scene came into view, she cued her mic. "ETA less than three minutes."

"Roger," Drake replied.

The interstate had been shut down by the state patrol, providing a nice open area to land the chopper. She kept the blades whirling as Drake and Kate jumped out. Within seconds they were running with the gurney between them to the scene were several ambulances were parked with their red lights flashing like a beacon.

The minutes dragged by slowly. This was the hardest part, waiting while the providers took care of stabilizing the patient that needed to be transferred.

Her stomach rolled a bit. Not bad enough that she thought she'd lose her lunch, but definitely annoying. She kept her gaze focused on the scene before her, peering through the midst of emergency personnel.

There! She saw Drake's tall frame and dark hair as he and Kate rolled the gurney toward the helicopter. She couldn't tell much about their fifty-two-year-old patient as he was covered with warm blankets up to his chin. As they drew closer, she could tell the patient had a breathing tube in place, as Drake was giving breaths with an Ambu bag.

There was a keen sense of urgency as Drake slid the patient in through the back hatch, then ran around to jump in. Even Kate, who normally talked nonstop, regardless of how awake or alert their patient happened to be, was unusually quiet as she and Drake focused on patient care.

"All set?" Megan asked once they were all tucked inside the bird.

"Yes." Drake's voice was curt. "Kate, keep an eye on that chest tube output. If it increases, let me know and we'll hang another unit of O blood."

"Will do," Kate responded.

Megan cued the paramedic base. "This is Lifeline, requesting permission to take off with patient needing to get to Trinity Medical Center."

"Lifeline, this is the paramedic base. You are clear to go."

"Ten-four." Megan swept her gaze over the area, making note of the power lines before lifting the chopper up off the ground and banking to the right toward Trinity Medical Center.

"Drake? The chest tube drainage container is almost full." Kate's voice held a note of anxiety.

"Let's hang the unit of blood and run the lactated ringers wide open." Drake's voice oozed confidence. "I'll swap over the chest tube drainage system."

Megan saw another mallard duck flying near the left side of the chopper. What was with the ducks flying around lately? This wasn't normally something she saw in December.

Then again, the weather was warmer than normal too. Maybe the ducks were confused and thought spring was coming.

The ride to Trinity didn't take long, and she soon had the chopper settled on the rooftop landing pad. A gust of wind hit just as she was bringing the chopper down, causing the bird to land with a jarring thud.

"Sorry, wind caught the blades on that one." She felt the need to explain that it wasn't her technique.

"Understood." Drake's smooth voice washed over her. "Kate, bag him for me while I go around back."

She listened as they worked together to get the trauma patient out of the bird and into the hospital where the trauma team and cardiac surgeon was waiting to take over. She'd understood from the conversation that the patient's bleeding hadn't slowed despite their efforts.

Figuring they'd be a while, Megan shut down the chopper and drew in a deep breath to ward off another wave of nausea. Flying was in her blood, from the time she was a teenager and her dad had allowed her to take private flying lessons through her four-year stint in the Air Force.

But now her stomach didn't seem to care for it. Or maybe it was the baby that didn't like it. She thought about the half of her grilled cheese sandwich and the single cheese and cracker square she had stored in the mini fridge of the pilot's room. Maybe when they returned to the hangar she could try eating her leftovers to see if that helped.

Or made things worse.

It was a fifty-fifty toss-up either way.

After ten minutes passed, she began to worry. Something must be wrong. Usually, the team returned to the chopper quickly in case another call came in.

Fifteen minutes. Eighteen.

Twenty-two minutes later, the door opened and Kate and Drake came toward the chopper. From the grim expressions on their faces, the news wasn't good.

She waited until they were seated and connected to the intercom system before asking, "What happened?"

"He didn't make it." Drake's voice was low and husky, as if he were taking the loss of their patient personally. "We took him straight to the OR, and when they opened his chest, he went into asystole. They tried to resuscitate him but without success."

Her chest tightened with empathy. "I'm sorry."

"Yeah." Drake blew out a breath. "Me too."

"Hey, it's not our fault, Drake." Kate's normally cheerful tone was subdued. "We kept him stable long enough to get him here."

"I know. But the end result is the same."

There was a long moment of silence before Megan cleared her throat. "Paramedic base, this is Lifeline. We're returning to the hangar, over."

"Ten-four, Lifeline."

No one spoke as she lifted the chopper airborne and made the short trip back to the hangar.

Logically, she knew they couldn't save everyone, especially trauma calls. But she could tell Drake was taking this one hard.

As much as she wanted to follow him into the lounge to make sure he was okay, her stomach dipped and turned, forcing her into the pilot's room to pull out her sandwich.

Apparently, battling never-ending nausea with food was her new normal.

And a long seven months yet to go.

THE CHEST PATIENT, Jimmy Paulson, wasn't even close to being like his wife, but seeing the crash scene, so similar to the one that had stolen Serena and Lance, had shaken Drake to the core.

Serena had hit a semitruck too. She'd been wearing her

seatbelt the same way Jimmy had been, but she had died anyway, the same way Jimmy had.

He dropped onto the sofa and held his head in his hands for a long moment. Thankfully, Kate didn't try to cheer him up or talk to him.

They had two long hours left of their twelve-hour shift. He found himself hoping there wouldn't be another call until the night crew had arrived.

Just three weeks to go in his Lifeline rotation. He'd learned a lot and valued the experience. Yet he hadn't anticipated that going out to various trauma scenes would remind him of Serena and Lance. It was very different being out on the interstate at the crash scene than having these patients rolling in through the doors of the ER.

Part of the memory might be the fact that the anniversary of their deaths loomed before him. At least he was working the weekend. Hopefully being busy would keep him from wallowing in the past.

"Drake? You okay?"

He sighed and lifted his head. He should have known Kate wouldn't hold off for long. "Yes, fine. It's just been a long day."

"Are you sure you don't want to play gin rummy?" She smiled and held up the deck of cards. "It will take your mind off things."

"I'm sure." He thought again about the email from the Find Your Family site. "I, uh, have some other work I need to take care of."

"Okay." She sat down at the table and began playing a game of solitaire. With actual playing cards rather than on a computer. He couldn't remember the last time he'd watched anyone do that, most people preferred to use their phone or tablet to play games.

Whatever. He rose to his feet and walked back over to the computer on the desk. Without enthusiasm, he typed in his username and password, bringing up his work email first to see if there was anything needing his attention, then switching over to his personal email.

The unread message was still there, the boldness akin to a neon light screaming *Read me!*

He moved the mouse and hovered over the email. He clicked it, and the message opened.

Dear Drake, I know this may come as a shock, but I'm your birth mother.

The words slammed into him, stealing his breath. No way. This couldn't be happening.

Could it?

Before he could read the rest, their pagers went off.

Relief warred with stark disappointment as he once again hastily shut down the computer. The call was a request for an ICU to ICU transfer, but he inwardly groaned when he realized the destination was Green Bay.

"Ready?" Kate asked, looping the handle of their supply bag over her shoulder.

"Yep." He stood and followed Kate into the debriefing room. Megan was seated in front of the radar screen, a frown on her face.

"I'm not sure we should take this call." She turned to look at him, then at Kate. "The winds are now forty miles per hour. Green Bay is a long trip, with uncertain weather conditions. It's already dark outside, I'd like to hold off for now."

He could tell Megan was worried about making the call to go to red flying conditions. "I'll contact the doc in Green Bay, see what's going on with the patient."

Megan's light gray eyes filled with relief. "Please let me

know how that goes. Meanwhile, I'll contact the paramedic base, let them know we may be grounded for a while."

Drake nodded and went back into the lounge to make his call. It took him a full five minutes before he was on the phone with the provider requesting the transfer.

"This is Dr. Drake Thorton from Lifeline Air Rescue. We are concerned about flying north to Green Bay with forty-mile-per-hour winds. Fill me in on what's going on with your patient."

There was a slight hesitation. "I'm Dr. Lambert, and the request to go to Trinity Medical Center is per the family. The patient has suffered a stroke, and the son is a physician and is insisting he be flown to Trinity Medical Center immediately."

"Has the patient gotten TPA per protocol?"

"Yes. But it's bad. Honestly, I don't think a transfer is going to make much of a difference. The poor guy is seventy-nine and has significant deficits. The TPA didn't reverse the brain damage. If it were my dad, I'd go the palliative care route, but per the son, that's not an option. Frankly, he's being pretty unrealistic about his expectations that his father will survive this and be fine."

"I see." Drake knew this was a political issue more than anything. "Who is the son?"

"Jason Hammer, he's an orthopedic surgeon at Trinity Medical Center."

Great, just great. If they denied the transfer, then Jared would likely hear from the son. Yet flying in red conditions for a patient that likely wouldn't benefit from the transfer put the crew at risk.

"Thorton? You still there?"

"I'm here." Drake raked his hand through his hair. "Listen, flying for over an hour in forty-mile-per-hour winds is not something to take lightly. I need to discuss this further with our medical director before I accept the transfer. And there's always ground transport, if they insist."

"Understandable." There was another pause before Lambert added, "The patient's son is willing to pay for the transfer even if the guy's insurance doesn't cover it."

"It's not a money issue," Drake said, even though he knew that receiving payments for services was important for the long-term viability of the ability to operate the Lifeline Air Rescue business. Budgets were always tight, and if the weather conditions weren't an issue, he'd be the first one to jump onto the helicopter to go to Green Bay.

"I just wanted you to know the son's position," Lambert said dryly. "Trust me, he's been pretty vocal about it."

Drake could only imagine. "I'll call you back." He disconnected from the line, then found Jared's cell phone. "Jared? Sorry to bother you, but we have a situation." He went on to explain the transfer request coming from an attending physician at Trinity Medical Center.

"We don't fly in red conditions, regardless of the request," Jared said firmly. "I'm not putting our crew at risk to appease a colleague. If the conditions change, then fine, we can go. But not until then."

"Thanks, Jared. I just thought it would be best to let you make the call as I'm sure you'll hear from this guy."

"Not a problem. I don't care if he calls me, we don't put three people at risk, four including his father, for no good reason. If the guy was thinking clearly, he'd realize how ridiculous that sounds."

He found himself smiling. "I couldn't agree more. Thanks, Jared."

The call to Dr. Lambert took longer because, of course, the patient's son wanted to talk to him personally. Drake drew in a deep breath and tried to be as diplomatic as possible.

"Yes, Dr. Hammer, I understand the grave condition your father is in. But transporting your father in forty-mile-per-hour winds for well over an hour puts him at risk too."

"I demand you pick up my father immediately!"

He rolled his eyes and tried again. "Dr. Hammer, you have three options here. One is to stay in Green Bay where Dr. Lambert can continue to provide excellent care—"

"Unacceptable," Hammer snapped.

"Second option is ground transport. It will take longer but without putting your father and an entire crew at risk. And third," he quickly added, before the idiot could say anything more, "is to wait a few hours to see if the weather conditions change. Once it's safe to fly, we're happy to do the transport. Your choice, Dr. Hammer."

"I'll find someone else to fly him if you won't."

"That's fine, we can certainly cancel the transfer on our end." Drake didn't hesitate to call his bluff.

There was a long silence, and he felt bad for Lambert having to deal with this guy. "We'll use ground transport, then. Thanks for nothing."

The phone went dead in his ear.

"Gee, that went well." Drake replaced the receiver in its cradle.

"You'd better warn Jared," Megan said from the doorway. She had clearly been listening to his side of the conversation.

"Already did." He shrugged. "Jared is fine with not going to Green Bay in red conditions."

Megan nodded, her expression grave. "Do you think I'm overreacting? Because of . . ." She gestured to her belly.

"No." He crossed over to her. "You're a good pilot, Megan.

Don't question your instincts. We're no good to anyone if we crash along the way."

She nodded yet didn't look entirely convinced. He longed to put his arm around her shoulders to comfort her, but Kate chose that moment to come in to join them.

He stepped back, thinking it was a good thing he was off the next day. This attraction to Megan was messing with his head.

As if the email from a woman claiming to be his birth mother hadn't knocked him off balance enough.

5

By the time the night shift arrived to relieve Megan and the rest of the crew, a low-hanging fog had settled over the city, prohibiting all transfers and trauma calls.

It made her feel better about putting off the Green Bay transfer. It wouldn't have been good to have gone all the way there only to experience the fog rolling in on their return trip.

"Ready to go?" Drake came up to stand beside her.

She stared at him in confusion. "Go where?"

He gestured to the door. "I'll walk you to your car."

"Are you afraid I'm going to fall flat on my face again?"

She pulled on her Lifeline jacket and picked up her purse.

"Not at all, it's just a safety measure."

Ironic that Drake didn't see the need to walk Kate out to her car. But refusing an escort seemed childish, so she fell into step beside him. Approaching the parking lot, she was surprised to realize how low the fog ceiling hung. Visibility was less than a quarter mile by her estimation.

Driving in the pea soup was only slightly safer than flying in it.

And when she saw Kate get into a waiting vehicle, leaning over to kiss the driver, she understood that the flight nurse didn't need an escort. Her physician husband had picked her up.

More proof that she shouldn't read more into Drake's actions than sheer polite kindness.

He'd have done the same for anyone. Something she needed to remember despite her hormone issues.

"This is it," she said, gesturing to her nondescript sedan. It wasn't old or particularly new, but it was paid for and that was all that mattered. "Thanks again."

"You're welcome." Drake stood there for a long moment, his hands tucked into the pockets of his Lifeline jacket as he waited for her to get in behind the wheel.

"Bye." She lifted her hand in a wave. "Have a nice day off."

"You too. See you Saturday."

They were scheduled to fly together again? Oh boy. She started her car and rolled out of the parking lot at a slow pace. Thankfully, the apartment building she lived in wasn't very far away. She'd learned many of the residents and nurses lived there because of the close proximity to both Trinity Medical Center and Children's Memorial Hospital.

Thankfully, she hadn't run into Drake and sincerely hoped she wouldn't. When she caught a glimpse of twin headlights piercing the fog behind her, she wondered if he was following her or if he did in fact live in the Red Oak Terrace apartment complex.

She pulled in and parked in the first available spot. Drake's vehicle sat waiting for her to go inside, before swinging around the parking lot and leaving.

A guy who takes his duty seriously. She shouldn't be touched by the action, but she was. It seemed now that Cal was out of her life she was being shown how wrong he'd been for her anyway.

A lesson better learned now than after they were married.

She put her hand over her abdomen as she walked up the stairs to her second-floor apartment. Thinking of Cal made her realize she should try to reach him one more time. If nothing else, to be sure he knew he had a child. If he didn't want anything to do with having a baby, then fine. So be it. It wasn't as if she needed his money. But she wasn't going to be accused of keeping her pregnancy a secret.

She wondered how First Lieutenant Emily Forbes would feel about the news. Would she be upset at Cal? Or stick by him? Not her problem, but she was curious.

After unlocking her door and shucking off her jacket, she shot the dead bolt home and went into the kitchen to find something to eat.

A bowl of chicken noodle soup and a half dozen crackers made her feel better. She opened her laptop and signed into her email. Still nothing from Cal.

She sent another message, telling him again, that she wanted him to know she was pregnant with their child. If this didn't work, maybe she'd give up and accept the fact that Cal had no desire to be a part of his son's or daughter's life.

Yes, it made her sad. Easier for her in the long run? Probably. But sad just the same.

The following morning an intense bout of nausea had her rushing into the bathroom first thing. She tried her best to keep from throwing up but lost the battle. Feely shaky and weak, she managed to drag herself into the kitchen long enough to make herself a cup of herbal tea and eat another cracker. But her stomach didn't settle.

Was Drake right about needing to take a leave of absence from work? What if she was this sick Saturday morning when she needed to be able to fly? How long would the morning sickness last anyway? She thought most women felt better by their second trimester.

The churning in her stomach intensified. She bolted to the bathroom again, and within minutes, the cracker made a return trip. Megan took a sip of cool water, rested her forehead against the cool porcelain, and tried not to panic. She'd read up on pregnancy, knew being sick was part of the deal, but this was so much worse than the previous day.

Every time she tried to leave the bathroom another bout of vomiting forced her back. After an hour, the panic she'd managed to keep at bay threatened to overwhelm her.

Her mind whirled. What if this was something more than pregnancy? What if she'd actually come down with the flu?

She curled up on the cold hard bathroom floor, wishing she could go to sleep until the virus—if that's what was going on—had run its course. But her stomach continued to clench and spasm. Until she thought she might die right here on her bathroom floor.

From somewhere in her apartment, her cell phone rang. She ignored it, unable to drag herself up and off the floor. But the caller persisted. Holding a towel to her face, heaven knew there wasn't much left in her stomach to come back out anyway, she crawled to her bedroom.

The phone was on her nightstand, still connected to the charger. She didn't recognize the number but answered it anyway.

"Hello?" Her voice was little more than a hoarse croak.

"Megan? It's Drake. You sound funny. Are you okay?"

Drake? She stared stupidly at the wall. She had no idea how he'd gotten her number or why he'd called, but at the moment she didn't care. "No. Sick."

"You're sick? Throwing up, sick?"

"Yes." Speaking was an effort, but she pushed the words past her throat.

"Do you have any sports drinks on hand? Something with electrolytes and sugar?"

"No." Her mind was fuzzy, his words seemingly coming from far away. "Sick," she repeated. "Flu."

"I'll be right there. What apartment number?"

She closed her eyes, both relieved and mortified that he was coming to help her. Her stomach spasmed again, and she pressed the towel to her mouth. After a moment she answered, "206."

"I'll be right there. Make sure the door is unlocked."

"'Kay." She heard the line go dead and set the phone back down on her nightstand. She should change out of her Christmas holly-patterned flannel pajamas but didn't have the strength. As it was, it took every ounce of energy she possessed to drag herself across the floor to the living room and to pull herself up enough in order to unlock the door.

Her head hurt. Her stomach hurt. Her entire body throbbed as if she'd been used as a crash dummy.

She was back in the bathroom by the time Drake arrived. His dark eyes were full of concern when he leaned over her. "I'm going to start an IV, okay?"

"Huh?" Megan thought she must have heard him wrong.

"Dehydration makes the vomiting worse. You need fluids, as soon as possible."

She wasn't in a position to argue. Closing her eyes, she waited for Drake to get the supplies together when suddenly she was lifted up in his arms and carried into the living room.

"What?" She couldn't believe it when he gently set her down on the sofa. She was no lightweight, but Drake didn't seem to mind.

"I need your arm." He pushed up the sleeve of her flannel pajamas and smoothed his hand over the area in the crook of her elbow. "You are severely dehydrated, Megan. The IV fluids should help you to feel better."

"C-couldn't f-feel much w-worse." Speaking even a few words was an effort.

To Drake's credit, she barely felt the cold antiseptic, followed by the prick of a needle. Keeping her eyes closed made her head less dizzy, so she listened as Drake prepared her IV.

The fluid made her feel chilled. When she shivered, he threw a blanket over her. But the impact of receiving fluids didn't take long. The cramping in her stomach eased, and the pounding in her head receded. After a half hour, she opened her eyes and looked up at him. He stood next to the sofa holding the IV bag.

"Wow."

The corner of his mouth quirked up in a smile. "Yeah, it's amazing what nearly five hundred milliliters of IV fluid can do for you. But don't try to get up yet. I want you to keep resting until the entire liter has been infused."

"I—don't know what to say." She abruptly felt self-conscious about how she looked, bedraggled and pale, and she smelled, stinky and sour.

Cal had never seen her like this. If he had, maybe he'd have left a long time ago.

Obviously, she must be feeling better to care what Drake thought of her. Which was ridiculous. But now that her mind was clearing, she realized how crazy it was that Drake was here in her apartment, infusing IV fluids into a catheter in her left arm in the first place. "How did you know I needed help?"

He flushed and shook his head. "I didn't. I, um, wanted to talk to you about something, so I asked around for your cell number. But when I heard your voice, I knew something was wrong."

She frowned. "How?"

He shifted from one foot to the other, peering up at the IV bag he was holding up. She wondered if his arm was getting tired. He finally met her gaze. "I don't know, your voice was different from the way you normally sound at work."

"I see." She didn't really but decided it didn't matter. He was here, and she was feeling better.

For the second time in two days, Drake had come to her rescue.

And as nice as that was, she knew she couldn't allow herself to become accustomed to this. Once Drake was no longer at Lifeline, she'd be alone again.

MEGAN LOOKED BETTER. He still wanted the entire liter of fluid to be given but was reassured at how quickly she'd bounced back.

Far better than just two hours earlier. The way she'd looked curled into a ball on the bathroom floor had scared him to death. He'd hauled her into his arms, as much to reassure himself she was still alive as to move her into a more comfortable position on the sofa.

"I'm getting hungry," she confessed. "Any chance I can try eating a bit of cheese with a cracker?"

He nodded. "Give me a minute to find a way to hang this IV bag."

"I'll hold it."

Her offer was sincere, but he doubted she had the strength. Instead, he draped the IV bag over the back of her sofa, making sure there would be no air introduced into the line before heading into her small kitchen.

"I have some already cut up in the fridge."

"I see it." He pulled out the baggie, then found the half-empty sleeve of saltine crackers. He carried them back over to the sofa. "Here you go. Easy does it, okay?"

"Okay." She gingerly nibbled a cheese square sitting atop a cracker. He prayed the nourishment would stay down. He'd promised himself he'd try one liter of fluid, and if that didn't work, he would take her to the ER at Trinity Medical Center.

"Thanks, Drake." Her voice was soft. "I'm not sure what I would have done if you hadn't called."

And what if he hadn't made the call? He wanted to point out that she should have gotten to her phone and used 911 to get to the hospital, but he held his tongue. No doubt, she'd figured that out already. "I'm glad I was able to help."

She ate only one cracker, before setting the rest aside. "Stomach still isn't quite right."

"Must be the flu, although we can't rule out hyperemesis gravidarum."

"Like Princess Kate. If this is a fraction of how she felt, she deserves a medal for having three kids." A ghost of a smile flitted across her features. "I hope it's just the flu though. There'd be no way on earth I could work through what I experienced this morning."

He was glad she was able to admit it, even though it bothered him on some level to think about not flying with her anymore. Which was stupid because his rotation would be over as of January third regardless. "The flu has been going around and should only last a day or two."

"I guess." She grimaced. "I was hoping to be back to work tomorrow."

"You'd better take the weekend off." Again, the pang of disappointment was annoying. It wasn't the first weekend he'd work without having Megan as the pilot. "Your body needs to rest and recuperate, especially in your condition."

There was a long moment before she nodded. "Okay, I'll take off Saturday for sure. I need to let Jared know, though, so he can find a replacement."

"Sunday too." He narrowed his gaze in a stern look. "Doctor's orders."

She looked as if she wanted to argue but pressed her lips together and slowly nodded. "Fine. But if I'm better by Sunday and they can't find anyone to take my shift, I plan to go in."

"Reese or Nate will cover for you. It's not a big deal." At least he was fairly sure the two senior pilots would help out. They all seemed dedicated to the Lifeline mission of saving lives.

"There are FAA rules about how many hours a pilot can fly." Megan glanced up at the IV bag, then back at him. There was only about a hundred milliliters left to go. "And we have night shifts to cover as well."

"I know." There were rules about how many hours a resident could work, too, for the same reason. Patient safety had to be the number one priority. "Maybe we can work out a split shift on Sunday."

"That would be great." Megan sighed and rested her hand on her stomach. "I, uh, need to go to the bathroom."

"Okay." He clamped off her IV, then helped her stand. She was unsteady at first, but then was able to walk the short distance to the bathroom. He draped the IV bag over the edge of the sink before backing out. "Call if you need something."

Her cheeks went pink, but she nodded. He hovered outside the closed door, listening intently for any indication that she needed help.

As a physician, the sounds of her emptying her bladder, flushing the toilet, then washing her hands were very familiar. But when she emerged from the restroom, he could tell she was acutely embarrassed.

"Hey, what's wrong?" He injected a note of levity in his voice. "You don't appreciate my nursing skills?"

That made her laugh. "You're doing okay from what I can tell."

He picked up the IV bag and rested his free hand in the small of her back as she returned to the living room sofa. "You're almost finished," he said as he reopened the clamp on the IV tubing.

"Good."

"Is there anything else you'd like me to do for you before I leave?" He glanced around at the apartment. "Would you like me to make you something to eat? Eggs maybe?"

"Eww. No eggs." She put her hand over her stomach again. "Mind you, I used to love them. But right now the very scent of them makes me want to throw up."

"Okay, no eggs," he agreed. "I can make you another grilled cheese sandwich."

"As crazy as it sounds, I'd like that. For some reason cheese appeals to me more than anything else."

"Hey, whatever works, right?" Drake eyed the IV bag. "Once this is empty, I'll make your sandwich."

"Thanks." She offered a weary smile. "I feel terrible imposing on your day off."

"It's nothing." He waved away her concern. To be honest, he would rather be here with her than home alone. And wasn't that a kick in the pants? Normally he preferred being alone.

"What was it that you wanted to talk to me about?"

"Hmm?" He tore his gaze from the IV bag to meet hers. "What do you mean?"

"Earlier, you said you called because you wanted to ask me something. What was it?"

"Oh, that." He'd hoped she wouldn't remember what he'd said. The email from the woman named Jolene Nevin who thought she might be his mother had occupied his thoughts until the moment he understood Megan was sick. "It's nothing really."

"Sure, you can see me looking like a train wreck, but you can't confide in me?" There was a hint of hurt in her tone.

He let out his breath in a sigh. "Okay, here's the thing. I mentioned I was adopted, right?"

"Right." Megan's gaze oozed compassion. "I'm sure that must have been wonderful and difficult at the same time."

Not really wonderful, at least in his situation, although he knew others had much better experiences. "Yes, well, about fourteen months ago, I joined this online group called Find Your Family. Yesterday, a woman emailed me claiming she's my birth mother."

"Really?" Megan looked surprised, then wary. "Do you think she's for real?"

"I don't know." He stared for long moments as the IV bag slowly emptied of fluid. He clamped off the tubing to prevent any air from getting in the line, then knelt beside the sofa. "I can discontinue your IV now."

Megan watched as he pulled the IV catheter and held a small gauze over the puncture site. When her gaze met his, he found himself momentarily lost in the crystal depths.

The urge to pull her into his arms was so strong he had to force himself to look away.

In that moment, he knew his call to Megan about finding his birth mother had been nothing more than an excuse to see her outside of work.

The acknowledgment scared him to the depths of his soul. Here he was playing nursemaid to a beautiful woman with the sexiest voice on the planet, even though he wasn't ready to replace Serena and Lance in his memories or in his heart.

6

Megan spent the next two days resting and recovering from her viral illness. Her bouts of morning sickness didn't go away, but she was feeling much better by the time she needed to head to Lifeline for her Tuesday shift.

She entered the Lifeline hangar, once again sipping her chamomile tea. Her usual breakfast of mild cheddar cheese and saltine crackers was in her purse. She'd brought twice as many as last time, hoping the rations would hold her over throughout her shift.

Seated at the debriefing table, Drake raked his gaze over her, nodding in approval and offering a faint smile at her improved condition. She found herself smiling back, despite her acute embarrassment at how he'd seen her at her worst. But looking back, she wasn't sure what would have happened if he hadn't arrived to provide IV fluids. A trip to the hospital at the very least.

Harm to her unborn child at the worst.

And after the way he'd rescued her and kept in touch

over the weekend between flight calls, she had to admit they were now friends.

Certainly closer than she'd allowed herself to be with any of the other residents who came through Lifeline.

"There's a pending transfer from Appleton." Flight nurse Kristin Page yawned and blinked to ward off a wave of exhaustion. Kristin and her fiancé, Dr. Holt Baxter, had obviously worked the night shift. Paramedic Ivan Ames was seated beside Drake, the two of them making up the daytime crew. The off-going pilot, Dirk Smith, also looked exhausted.

"What are the details on the transfer?" Drake asked.

Holt leaned forward. "It's a potential liver transplant recipient, guy by the name of Mike Miller. Flying conditions were iffy this morning because of the fog, but it's supposed to clear in the next hour."

"Okay." Drake nodded. "Sounds good."

Megan took a seat beside Dirk, who was the oldest pilot on staff at Lifeline. "How are the winds?"

"Minimal at ten miles per hour. The fog was the biggest concern, the weather has been so crazy mild, it's more like spring out there than winter." Dirk shrugged. "Should clear up without a problem though."

She nodded, knowing he was probably right. Patchy areas of fog weren't enough to go from yellow flying conditions to red. Watching the radar for a long moment, she found herself hoping the day would stay busy. Maybe so much so that she wouldn't have time to talk to Jared later that morning about her condition.

As if on cue, her stomach clenched and rolled. Ugh. She rose and moved into the pilot's room to discreetly pull a cheesy saltine cracker from her bag.

A sip from her sports drink also helped. Drake had

taught her the importance of keeping hydrated and your electrolytes in balance. Her throwing up was far less when she took small sips of a sports drink throughout the day.

She wrinkled her nose at the taste but told herself to get over it. Better to force it down than to have her breakfast, lunch, and dinner come up.

The murmur of voices from the debriefing room faded away. The night shift crew must have headed home. She finished her cracker and returned to the debriefing room to check on the weather.

Drake was still there, sipping coffee. "You look great."

She blushed, reminding herself that great was relative to the way he'd seen her last, which likely resembled roadkill. "Thanks. I've been sipping sports drinks the way you suggested which has helped a lot."

"I'm glad." He smiled and gestured to the radar screen. "Will you let us know when we're cleared to fly? The hospital in Appleton called and requested an updated ETA."

She scrolled through computer screens providing images of various weather patterns. The equipment was high-end, very similar to what the Air Force used. "I think we can go anytime. The dense fog has lifted, leaving just a few patches here and there. Most of which we can fly above."

Drake nodded. "Okay, I'll let them know."

When he rose to his feet, she said, "What did you decide to do about the email?"

He hesitated. "So far I haven't done anything. I know I should respond, but the weekend was busy here, and I ended up spending my day off getting caught up on errands."

"Understandable." She was secretly pleased that despite his errands, he'd called to check on her. Twice. And maybe a teeny tiny bit disappointed that he hadn't stopped by on Monday during his day off. "Let me know if you want to talk it through before you respond."

He shrugged as if it wasn't a big deal when she knew it was a very big one. "I will, thanks. If we're clear to fly, I need to call the provider at Appleton to let him know."

"Okay. I'll get the chopper ready." Megan headed out to the hangar and went through the preflight checklist before pulling the bird out of the hangar. Drake and Ivan joined her a few minutes later. Ivan had the duffel bag of supplies slung over his shoulder.

She climbed into the pilot's seat as the two men got settled in the back. After receiving permission from the paramedic base to take off, she lifted the chopper off the ground and into the air.

Keeping an eye on the foggy areas, she took the bird high enough to avoid the worst of it. The sky looked as if it would clear by midmorning, which was good news if she wanted to be busy enough to postpone her conversation with Jared.

The flight to Appleton was uneventful from her perspective, but she could tell by the conversation Drake had with Charles Forte, the provider in Appleton, their patient wasn't doing well.

She cued her mic. "ETA less than three minutes."

"Roger," Drake replied.

After executing a smooth landing, Drake and Ivan jumped out and hurried inside. She kept the blades whirling even though she sensed it would take longer than usual for Drake and Ivan to return. The sicker the patient, the more they tended to make sure everything was in order prior to the transfer.

"Lifeline, this is paramedic base, do you copy?"

"Ten-four, this is Lifeline. What's up?"

"The wind has shifted, bringing more fog in from Lake Michigan. It's not bad, but we wanted to update you on the flying conditions."

She drew in a deep breath and let it out slowly. "Roger, base, appreciate the information. What's the visibility?"

"About a half mile, so as I said, not terrible. Could dissipate by the time you arrive."

"Roger that." She clicked off and put her hand over her stomach. The nausea had returned. Might have been good to bring the sports drink along for the ride.

Next time. And she'd bring the cheese and crackers along too.

A full fifteen minutes passed before Ivan and Drake emerged from the hospital with their patient on the gurney between them. She informed the paramedic base of their imminent takeoff as the two men hefted the guy into the back of the chopper, then joined him in the back.

"Ten-four, Lifeline, you're cleared to go."

She maneuvered the chopper upward, taking note of the extra weight that caused a bit of a drag. She cued the mic. "How much does our patient weigh?"

"One hundred and sixty kilos according to the provider," Drake responded. "I know it's close to the max capacity we can take, but he's in rough shape and really needs to get to Trinity Medical Center."

"Okay." No question they'd use more fuel on this trip, but she trusted Drake's judgment. If this guy needed to get to Trinity, then she was determined to make that happen.

For the next ten minutes it was smooth sailing.

"Drake? Check out his stomach, I think it's more bloated than it was when we took off."

Megan tensed, keeping her eyes peeled for birds and

drones as she listened to the two men in back discuss their patient's change in condition.

"Get me a nasogastric tube." Drake's voice was urgent. "I hope he's not bleeding into his gut."

Her own stomach clenched at the idea, and she swallowed hard, praying she wouldn't throw up if their patient did.

"There, get the suction." Drake must have placed the tube.

"I'm getting blood from his stomach." Ivan's tone was grim. "This isn't good."

Megan cued her mic. "Do you want me to divert back to Appleton? We're not quite at the halfway point."

There was a moment of hesitation before Drake responded. "No, I say we push forward. We're infusing blood and starting him on a medication to clamp down the bleeding vessels."

"Okay, but you need to know there's more fog in Milwaukee now. Apparently the wind has shifted, bringing more moisture in from the lake."

"What do you think, Megan?" Drake asked. "This is your call."

She hesitated only a moment. "I think we'll be fine. All this discussion has pushed us past the halfway point anyway, so it would take longer to turn around and go back than to get to Trinity. I just won't be able to increase our speed as much as I'd like given the weight we're carrying."

"Understood. Ivan? Get another container, that one is nearly full."

A full container wasn't good news, but Megan stayed focused on her job, which was flying. As she closed the gap between Appleton and Milwaukee, she noticed a large patch of fog looming up ahead. She cut through it without difficulty, but then she saw additional clouds of fog all around her.

"Base, this is Lifeline. I'm changing my approach to come in from the west, over."

"Ten-four, Lifeline. You're cleared to approach from the west."

It was the only thing she could think of to avoid the worst of the fog. But the tactic didn't change the fact that the hospital's landing pad was located a mere ten miles from the lakeshore.

Another area of fog obscured her vision. Using her control panel as a guide, she stayed on course, breathing a sigh of relief when the fog cleared enough that she could pinpoint the lights of the landing pad.

"ETA less than three minutes." She wanted to let the flight crew know they were close, especially since she knew their patient was in a precarious situation.

As she lowered the chopper, another cloud of fog came straight toward them. She held her breath, her mind rapidly going through her options.

Land blind or go back up for another circle around the landing pad?

Up. She pulled the stick, bringing the bird back upward, and banked to the left.

"We're losing his pressure," Ivan said.

"I know. Megan? I thought we were about to land?" Drake's urgent tone made her feel guilty.

"We are." She gritted her teeth and made the loop around the landing pad, coming in again from the west. The fog was still hovering over the area but had faded enough to provide a bit of visualization down below. Not much, but enough to glimpse the landing pad.

Sending up a silent prayer for God to watch over them,

she guided the chopper down to the landing pad, hitting it with more force than normal. Maybe because of the added weight, but more likely because of her obscured vision.

"All clear," she said through the microphone.

The crew didn't waste any time. They'd already called for a hot unload, so the medical team was waiting to meet them. The chopper bounced a bit when they removed their large patient and wheeled him across to the doorway.

Megan loosened her deathlike grip on the stick, shut down the engines, and bowed her head.

Difficult landings weren't uncommon in the Air Force, but here in the civilian world these sorts of events were taken seriously. In combat, you had little choice but to fly into danger. Here, they always had a choice and making the wrong one put not only their patient but their entire crew at risk.

And this choice had nearly been a disaster.

DRAKE GRATEFULLY HANDED the care of their very sick patient over to the critical care team. The guy was too sick, and frankly too large, to be a viable candidate for a liver transplant, but at this point, keeping him alive long enough to see another day was his only concern.

He and Ivan stayed for a few minutes longer as the critical care team implemented the massive transfusion protocol and inserted a Sengstaken-Blake tube to put pressure against the bleeding esophageal varices. It occurred to him that maybe this transfer had been too high of a risk to take in the first place. He needed to talk it through with Jared to make sure he wasn't overreacting.

Megan had done an amazing job of getting them all here

in one piece. But had it been necessary to go at all? The moment he'd seen the guy's body habitus, Drake had doubted the provider's claim of this patient being placed on the liver transplant list. And the way his condition had deteriorated over the flight back to Milwaukee confirmed his suspicions.

The guy was too sick to tolerate such a complicated surgery.

"Come on, Ivan. Megan's waiting."

"Yeah, okay." Ivan dragged himself away from the procedure going on at the bedside. Between them they pushed the Lifeline gurney back through the ICU and up the elevator to the rooftop landing pad.

Coming out into the cold December air, he stopped abruptly when he realized the chopper wasn't running. Megan? His heart thudded painfully as he abandoned the gurney and sprinted over to the helicopter.

He wrenched open the door. "What's wrong? Are you hurt? Sick?"

She lifted her head from her hands. She'd removed her helmet, which was tucked beside her. "I'm fine. It's just—that was rough."

It worried him that she'd thought the landing was rough. Had the situation been worse than he'd assumed? Granted, there hadn't been much time to wonder about Megan's landing skills as he and Ivan fought to keep their patient alive.

"You sure you're okay?" He wanted to pull her out of the seat and into his arms, but of course that would be inappropriate.

"Fine." She forced a smile. "How's our patient?"

He grimaced. "Not great, but in good hands."

"What's going on?" Ivan came over to join them. Drake

took a step back, hoping his feelings toward Megan weren't telegraphed on his features.

"Everything is fine. I shut down the chopper because I didn't want to waste fuel. We used more than normal by carrying the extra weight."

"Okay." Ivan's curious gaze bounced between Drake and Megan, but he didn't push. "I'll get the gurney in the back."

Drake moved away, giving Megan room to close the door. She waited until they were settled in their respective seats before donning her helmet and firing up the chopper.

"Base, this is Lifeline requesting a stop to refuel and then to return to the hangar."

"Ten-four, Lifeline, you're clear. The fog has been dissipating so shouldn't be a problem."

"Roger." Megan's voice was calm as she lifted the bird into the sky. The trip to refuel didn't take long, and from there they returned to the hangar. Peering out the window, Drake noted the fog was definitely lighter.

At the Lifeline hangar, Ivan took their duffel of supplies inside to restock, leaving Drake to clean up the interior of the chopper with bleach. He was keenly aware of how Megan walked around the chopper, intently checking it over to make sure their hard landing hadn't caused a problem.

After finishing the interior, he jumped down to join her. "How does it look?"

"Okay, although I'd like Mitch to take a peek as well, just to be sure."

Drake knew Mitch was the Lifeline mechanic. "Probably a good idea. Do we need to go on red flying status until he does?"

She slowly nodded. "Yeah. It's for the best."

He rested his hand on her shoulder. "How are you, really?"

Her gray eyes clashed with his. "Fine. This is what I get paid to do."

"But it's different when you have another life to be concerned about, isn't it?"

She looked away, staring out at the cloudy sky. "I'm not the first pregnant pilot or crew member on the planet. It's all part of the job."

Again, he wanted to draw her close, to find a way to reassure her he understood what she was going through. But Jared took that moment to come outside.

"I heard about the landing." Their bosses gaze raked over them. "Everyone okay?"

"Yes, but I'd like to talk to you about this latest transfer when you have a minute. I'm not sure the requesting facility was completely honest with us."

Jared's gaze widened in surprise. "Why is that?"

Drake hesitated, not sure he should have this conversation out here. "The guy was close to our maximum weight capacity for one thing, and the provider in Appleton claimed the patient was to be listed for a liver transplant."

Jared's gaze narrowed. "Not if he's at the high level of our weight limit."

"Exactly. And he started bleeding from his esophagus ten minutes into the flight. No way was he stable enough to be considered for a liver."

"Hmm." Jared nodded thoughtfully. "I appreciate your insight on this. I'll make a couple of calls to see if I can verify the story. At the very least, these outside hospitals need to understand we have a weight limit for a helicopter for a reason. It's not to be picky, it's to make sure everyone stays safe."

"Agreed." Drake was relieved to know Jared agreed with his assessment. "Thanks."

Jared nodded. "Not a problem." He turned toward Megan. "Do you have time to talk?"

Megan abruptly shook her head and ran into the hangar as if a rabid dog was after her.

"What in the world?" Jared stared after her, flabbergasted. "What was that about?"

Drake hesitated. Megan's secret wasn't his to tell, but it was only a matter of time before the entire crew caught on to her frequent and hurried trips to the bathroom.

"Um. . ." He shrugged. "You need to ask Megan."

Jared crossed his arms over his chest. "I'm asking you, Thorton. I know she had the flu, but I thought she was better."

Drake let out a sigh. "She doesn't have the flu."

"Then what?"

He really, really didn't want to be the one to tell him. But it was clear Jared wasn't going to let him out of this.

He stalled, the seconds ticking by slowly. Jared didn't move, clearly expecting an answer.

"I'm pregnant." Megan's voice coming from behind Jared saved Drake from having to break his promise.

Amazingly, Jared didn't look surprised. Maybe because he had two kids of his own. Their medical director nodded, turned to face her, then gestured toward the building. "Let's meet in my office."

Megan fell into step beside him as they headed inside. Drake wanted to join them but knew Jared wouldn't allow it.

What happened next was between the two of them. Boss and employee.

Drake dropped into a chair and scrubbed his hands over his face. For someone who was finishing their last few weeks at Lifeline, he cared more about what was going on behind closed doors than he had a right to.

7

Megan sat across from Jared with her stomach tied in knots that had nothing to do with her pregnancy. Her cheeks were flushed with embarrassment, although she knew Jared wouldn't pass judgment on her.

She was doing enough of that on her own.

"How far along are you?"

"I'm not exactly sure, roughly twelve weeks. I haven't been to the OB yet, my appointment is a week from today, the first Monday after Christmas."

Jared nodded, his gaze sympathetic. "Morning sickness?"

"Yes, but over the weekend I had the flu as well." She decided there was no point in putting off the inevitable. "I take full accountability for the hard landing. I don't think the chopper has been impacted, but I'd like Mitch to look her over just to be sure."

"What role did the fog play in the landing?" Jared's tone was calm and rational.

She frowned. "It played a role, but it was my decision not to turn back to Appleton when I noticed a change in the weather conditions." She drew in a deep breath. "I take full responsibility for my actions. If that means losing my job, then fine."

"What are you talking about?" Jared's brows levered upward. "You're not going to lose your job. I'm well aware of the risk we take flying on a daily basis. I value you as a member of our team, Megan."

Tears pricked her eyes, which was crazy because she wasn't the crying sort. She'd survived basic training and keeping up with the other flyboys in the Air Force. Not once did she let them see her upset, no matter how derogatory the comments.

But now, Jared's kindness and understanding caused the waterworks to flow.

Stupid hormones.

"I'm glad to hear that, but I feel terrible about putting the crew and the patient at risk."

"And yourself, along with your baby," Jared pointed out. He waved an impatient hand. "Stop beating yourself up over this. We can't control the weather, no matter how much we try to be prepared. However, I would like to know from your doctor how long you'll be able to fly so I can make arrangements for a temporary replacement."

Replacement.

The word hung in the air between them. It was only right that Jared would bring someone in to cover her shifts, but the idea of being replaced to the point she wasn't needed any longer terrified her.

"I'd like to fly as long as possible," she said, breaking the silence. "I was hoping to talk to my doctor before bringing this to you. Unfortunately, the bouts of morning sickness are difficult to hide. Drake figured it out, and it was only a matter of time before the others did as well."

Jared's lips twitched in a smile. "I suspected you were pregnant, you bolted past us like a woman with her hair on fire. Shelly was the same way with our baby." His gaze softened when he spoke of his wife and family, they had a son Ty, who was really Jared's nephew, but had welcomed a baby girl not long ago. "And don't worry about the flight suit, I think we have a couple of two-piece pregnancy flight suits Shelly created that you can wear when you start to show."

"We do?" She'd never heard of such a thing. "Um, okay. Thanks."

Jared leaned forward, resting his elbows on his desk. "Do you need additional help? Is the baby's father supporting you?"

Drake was the only one who'd been supporting her on an emotional level, but she didn't dare say that out loud. "No, sir. The baby's father is currently stationed overseas and hasn't acknowledged my emails to him."

Jared scowled. "I'll reach out to him."

"No, really, it's okay." The idea of her boss taking on the role of aggrieved father was too much to bear. "He could be off on a mission without computer access. I'm bound to hear from him sooner or later. But I'm doing okay financially." At least, she would be if she could work until her seventh month. Maybe even a little longer.

It wasn't as if she was flying to a place that didn't have medical help. Aside from trauma calls, which were mostly local, every transport was from a medical facility.

Of course, not all of them were equipped to deal with emergency pregnancy issues, but still, it wasn't as if she were in the middle of the forest with no physicians nearby.

Jared drummed his fingers on the desk as he considered her statement. "If you need assistance in getting his attention, let me know."

No way, she thought. But she smiled and said, "Thanks. I'm sure it will all work out."

Jared leaned back in his chair. "Get Mitch to check out the chopper. We'll hold off taking any calls until he's had a chance to look her over."

"I will." She stood and made her way back to the debriefing room. Drake was sitting there, waiting for her, but she reached for the phone to call the mechanic. Mitch promised to be there within ten minutes, so her next call was to the paramedic base to let them know about their red flying status. "We won't respond to any calls until the chopper has been checked over."

"Ten-four, Lifeline. Keep us posted."

"You okay?" Drake asked the moment she hung up the phone.

"Yes. Jared is a great boss."

"Very true," Drake agreed. "No flying restrictions?"

"Not unless they come from my doctor." She sat across from him, suddenly feeling exhausted. This constant desire for a nap had to be a side effect of being pregnant because normally she had trouble sleeping at night. The minute she crawled into bed was the time her brain decided to think and plan rather than relax.

"You did a good job with landing the helicopter, Megan. It was pea soup out there, but you brought us down safely."

She shook her head. "It would have been smarter to turn around and go back to Appleton until the weather cleared when I had the chance."

"Easy to say in hindsight. But at the time, you made the right decision. Both Ivan and I were in agreement on pushing forward."

She offered a lopsided smile. "Thanks for trying to make me feel better."

"I'm not." A flash of anger crossed his features. "I'm telling you the truth. I would tell you if I disagreed."

He would, she knew. Drake was not only honest but had integrity. Something that Cal seriously lacked. "You're right, I just don't like the idea of putting you, Ivan, and the patient at risk."

"We were safe in your hands." His confidence in her abilities was humbling. For a moment she simply looked at him, wondering how this had happened. How she'd grown close to one of the *rotating residents,* as she secretly called them, in such a short time.

She couldn't read his dark eyes, but there was no denying the tingling awareness shimmering between them. But the moment ended quickly when the door to the hangar banged open revealing Mitch.

"Arrived faster than anticipated," he announced. "I checked the bird—she's safe to fly. No stress on the struts that I can see. No reason to remain grounded from my perspective."

"Great." She reached for the phone. "I'll let the paramedic base know."

Mitch grabbed a cup of coffee, obviously intending to stick around for a bit. As she reset their flying to green status, Megan tried to ignore the way Drake's gaze followed her every move.

She didn't understand how he managed to make her feel like the most important person on the planet.

And worse was how much she liked it.

∼

DRAKE BATTED down a flash of annoyance at Mitch's interruption. It wasn't as if there was the expectation of privacy within the Lifeline hangar. In fact, there were always people coming and going, even while off duty.

He tore his gaze from Megan and told himself to get a grip. Hadn't he lost his wife and son? Hadn't he promised himself to dedicate himself to his career, instead of getting emotionally involved?

Yes, he had. So why was he sitting here, thinking of pulling Megan into his arms for a kiss?

He must be losing his mind.

Their pagers chirped in a simultaneous rhythm. His, Megan's and Ivan's from the lounge. He glanced down at the message, his gut clenching when he read the call.

Pregnant female estimated gestation of thirty-six weeks, with bleeding and suspected placenta previa requires urgent transport from Cedar Bluff Hospital to Trinity Medical Center.

An OB call. Great, just what he'd hoped to avoid near the anniversary of losing his wife and son. At least it wasn't a trauma OB call. Still, he knew he'd have to work hard to stay focused.

Last thing he needed was to suffer flashbacks to the horrible way he'd lost the two people he'd loved the most.

"Drake? Are you ready to go?" Ivan appeared in the debriefing room, the duffel bag of supplies he'd replenished from the previous call slung over his shoulder.

"Yes." He belatedly realized Megan had already gone out to the chopper. See? He was letting the past mess with his mind. He needed to let it go.

Drake followed Ivan to the chopper, climbing into the back behind the paramedic. Ivan had a lot of experience, but it was disconcerting to be the only physician miles in the air.

"Base, this is Lifeline, requesting permission to take off."

Megan's smooth lyrical voice wasn't enough to help him relax.

"Ten-four, Lifeline. You're cleared to go."

The chopper went vertical, banking to the right in a movement that now seemed natural to him. He thought about their patient. Placenta previa was a condition where the placenta covered the opening of the cervix so that the baby couldn't be born vaginally. There was an increased risk of bleeding along with the possibility of placenta abruption, a condition where the placenta breaks away from the uterine wall, causing excessive bleeding and a high risk of both maternal and fetal demise.

From what he remembered during his OB rotation, the latter usually happened earlier in the woman's pregnancy. Thirty-six weeks was far enough along for the fetus to survive.

Running through the facts in his mind helped keep him calm. He thumbed the intercom switch. "Base, this is Drake Thorton. I'd like to speak to the OB provider at Cedar Bluff."

"Ten-four, Dr. Thorton. Please hold." He waited for the paramedic base to patch him through to the small hospital located on the shores of the lakefront. "Dr. Thorton? I have Dr. Berkley on the line."

"Dr. Berkley, this is Drake Thorton requesting an update on Tiffany Lucinda, the patient with suspected placenta previa."

"Yes, Dr. Thorton, so far Tiffany is stable, the bleeding isn't too bad. Unfortunately Tiffany hasn't had any prenatal care, so we're in the process of obtaining an ultrasound to see exactly how bad this placenta previa is."

"Is she having any contractions?"

"No, so far she's been fine other than the bleeding."

Drake glanced at Ivan who was listening to the conversation. "Okay, thanks. I would appreciate receiving any ultrasound information you're able to obtain once we arrive."

"Of course, that's not a problem. We'll see you soon." Dr. Berkley disconnected from the call.

"Doesn't sound too bad," Ivan said with a wide smile. "We'll get her to Trinity without a problem."

Drake didn't answer but hoped and prayed Ivan was right. He watched for birds out the window, amazed at how the sky had cleared of the earlier fog, turning into a nice day.

"ETA seven minutes," Megan said.

"Ten-four." Drake was impressed with how well Megan was handling flying again after their hard landing. Her Air Force training had served her well.

Except for that idiot boyfriend of hers who'd run off and left her pregnant and alone. He wanted to smack some sense into the guy, yet he also didn't want Megan to take him back. Sure, the jerk had a right to see his kid if that's what he wanted, but Megan deserved so much better.

Megan brought them down onto the Cedar Bluff helipad in a landing that was smooth as silk. Drake followed Ivan out of the chopper and down to the back where they pulled the gurney out and then ran inside.

They had to follow the signs to the OB unit, as Ivan had never been there before. The walls were decorated with adorable baby photos that made his heart ache.

"Dr. Thorton?" He turned at the sound of his name. "I'm Dr. Berkley. Tiffany is this way."

Drake and Ivan pushed the gurney, following in Berkley's wake.

Tiffany was young, early twenties by his estimation, and looked pale and scared. He forced a reassuring smile.

"Hi, I'm Dr. Thorton and this is Paramedic Ames. We're going to be transporting you to Trinity Medical Center, okay?"

Tiffany paled. "I'm afraid of flying."

Oh boy. He glanced at Ivan, wondering what to say. Being in a commercial aircraft wasn't nearly as scary as being in a helicopter.

Not that he planned to tell Tiffany that.

"We can give you something to help you relax," Dr. Berkley said. "And you won't be in the air for long. Trust me, this is the safest way for you to get the help you need."

"I'll hold your hand the whole time," Ivan offered. "My wife is afraid to fly, too, but she's brave enough to go up in the air when needed."

Drake wasn't sure if that part was true or not, but Tiffany reluctantly nodded in agreement.

Ivan connected the equipment while Drake reviewed the recent lab results and the ultrasound images.

"The placenta isn't too bad, it's just the front edge here that overlaps the cervix." Berkley outlined the area with his fingertip. "I think she'll be fine until you get her to Trinity for a C-section."

Drake certainly hoped so. "Sounds good. Ivan? Do you need help with anything?"

"Nope, we're all set." They had similar monitoring equipment on the helicopter that most hospitals had, but without the added sounds. There was no way to check fetal heart tones by listening while they were in the back of a noisy chopper.

Visually monitoring the fetal heart tones would have to be good enough.

Once Tiffany was transferred onto the Lifeline gurney, they wheeled her to the elevator and up to the helipad.

"Too loud!" He could barely hear Tiffany scream over the whirling blades.

He and Ivan stored her in the back, then quickly ran around to join her. Ivan put the headphones on and took her hand in his.

"It's okay, see? We're fine in here. Dr. Thorton is going to watch you very closely as we get you to Trinity Medical Center."

"I'm scared." Tiffany clutched Ivan's hand in a white-knuckled grip.

Drake documented a set of initial vital signs, including taking note of the baby's heart rate of 164 beats per minute. He listened through his helmet as Megan took them airborne.

The trip between Cedar Bluff and Trinity Medical Center wasn't long, but as he was checking Tiffany, he noticed she was having more vaginal bleeding.

A cold sweat formed on the back of his neck, beads rolling down the inside collar of his flight suit. He cued his microphone to speak to their patient. "Tiffany, are you having any pain?"

"Some cramps." Her eyes were wide as she looked between him and Ivan. "I can tell we're up in the air. I feel sick."

"You're fine. We're going to be landing in less than fifteen minutes." He kept his voice soothing, but inside panic stabbed deep. What could he do to stop the bleeding?

Absolutely nothing.

He kept his gaze focused on the baby's heart rate. It was trending up a bit, and he wondered if mom's stress was being felt by the infant.

"Ivan, increase the IV rate from one hundred to one-fifty."

"Got it." Ivan didn't release his grip on Tiffany's hand as he increased the IV rate.

The baby's heart rate continued to climb. First to 170, then to 175.

"Megan? What's our ETA?"

"About eight minutes," Megan replied.

Eight minutes. He could keep Tiffany and her baby alive for the next eight minutes, right?

Right.

Was it possible Tiffany had broken her water without Dr. Berkley realizing it? An infection could also cause the baby's heart rate to increase, just like it did for kids and adults.

Or what if she was further along than what Berkley thought? He picked up the ultrasound again, peering closely at the infant's landmarks.

The baby looked to be about six pounds. A good size for thirty-six weeks.

"Ohhh, my cramping is getting worse." Tiffany's large eyes filled with tears. "Please. I don't want to have my baby in a helicopter."

Drake didn't want that either. He looked at the monitor and noticed she was indeed having contractions. "Megan? We need to get to Trinity ASAP."

"Roger. ETA less than five minutes."

Five minutes. He swallowed hard and gave Tiffany a reassuring smile. "You won't have this baby until we get to the hospital, okay?"

"Okay." Her gaze looked trustingly into his. Drake hoped and prayed he was right.

If she went into full-blown labor with the birth canal partially occluded by the placenta, both mother and baby might die.

The underlying note of fear in Drake's tone was a distraction Megan couldn't afford. The skies were clear now, no sign of the earlier fog, but she'd sweated the landing at Cedar Bluff.

It was getting back up to ride after falling off a horse, right? Except she'd never gone horseback riding in her life.

She cued her mic to let the base know she was approaching the landing pad at Trinity Medical Center. She wiped her damp palms on her flight suit and concentrated on executing a smooth landing.

It wasn't until after Drake and Ivan had gotten out of the chopper, retrieved their patient from the back hatch, and headed inside that she allowed herself to think about the conversation she'd overheard.

Contractions and bleeding didn't sound good. And there was likely more going on from a medical perspective that she didn't understand.

She rested her hand over her abdomen, thinking about her baby. Having been focused on her morning sickness and her future ability to fly, she hadn't really taken the time to embrace the fact that she was blessed to be creating a new life. A baby. A child.

The upcoming Christmas holiday was the perfect time to reflect on the miracle of Jesus's birth.

And her future with a new baby. Once her baby was born, roughly mid-June of next year, her life would change forever.

It was exciting and scary at the same time.

She was so lost in her thoughts that she didn't realize how much time had passed. A good fifteen minutes since landing, but no sign of Drake or Ivan.

Had something happened to their patient or her baby? She sincerely hoped not.

The seconds dragged by with agonizing slowness. When Drake and Ivan finally emerged from the doorway, she tried to read the expression on their faces.

Once they'd stored the gurney in the back and jumped in, she cued her mic. "Is Tiffany okay?"

"Yeah, Tiffany and her son are doing fine." Drake's voice held a note of exhaustion.

"She delivered already?" Once again, she found herself putting her hand over her abdomen as if to protect the baby growing within.

"They ended up doing a crash C-section the minute we rolled her in," Ivan explained. "It was touch and go for a minute there, they didn't even wait to take her off our gurney. Just did the surgery and then stabilized her bleeding. The little guy is doing okay, about six weeks early, but has a healthy pair of lungs on him."

A crash C-section. She swallowed hard, thinking about how close they'd come to potentially losing them both. "I'm glad to hear they're both doing all right."

"Trust me, I'm glad too," Drake said dryly. "I'd be happy

if I could spend the rest of my time here at Lifeline without another OB emergency."

She thought that was an odd statement for him to make but didn't say anything more. Instead, she told the paramedic base they were returning to Lifeline and was given permission to take off.

It wasn't until they were back at the Lifeline hangar that Megan realized she wasn't feeling sick to her stomach. She frowned, wondering if that was a good sign or something to be concerned about. The nausea had been her constant companion for so long it felt odd to feel normal.

Hungry, but without the sense of fearing if she didn't eat soon, she'd throw up.

"Anyone hungry for pizza?" Jared asked as he entered the debriefing room. "I'm buying."

"I'm in," Drake said with a weary smile. "I could use a carb load about now."

"I could eat," Megan agreed, hoping the spicy pizza wouldn't give her heartburn.

"Me too," Ivan added. "That last transfer was a tough one."

Jared frowned. "Everything go okay?"

"Yeah." Drake nodded. "Placenta previa case who began having contractions and bleeding during the transfer. When we arrived at Trinity Medical Center's labor and delivery department, they took one look at her and prepped her for an emergency C-section. Mom and baby boy are doing fine."

"Good work," Jared praised. "All the more reason to celebrate with pizza."

The conversation turned to the upcoming Christmas holiday. Ivan regaled them with stories about his young daughter's excitement on finding Eddie the Elf on the shelf every morning in a new place. The most ingenious being when Ivan had hung Eddie at the end of a ceiling fan pull cord.

"Do you know how hard it is to make Eddie the Elf look like he's flying rather than being strangled by a noose?" Ivan demanded. "It took me over an hour to get him situated up there."

Megan chuckled. "I hope you took a picture. Too funny."

Drake didn't say much but sipped coffee as they waited for the pizza to arrive. She wanted to ask Drake why he was so reticent about Christmas, but this wasn't really the time or place.

Jared joined them in the debriefing room, chatting as they dug into the two large pepperoni pizzas loaded with the works that Jared had paid for. She noticed all three of the guys waited until she said she was finished before polishing off the last of the meal.

"That was awesome, thanks, boss." Ivan grinned as he sat back in his chair.

"You're welcome." Jared rose to his feet. "I have more paperwork to get finished, then plan to head home. Let me know if you need anything."

"We'll be fine," Megan assured him.

Drake nodded in agreement, still unusually quiet. Granted, he'd been this way since beginning his Lifeline rotation in October, but lately he'd opened up a bit, at least with her.

Jared returned to his office, and Ivan went into the lounge claiming he had education modules to complete. Megan glanced at Drake, who stared broodingly off into the distance.

She reached over to rest her hand on his arm. "What is it?"

"Huh? Nothing." He seemed to shake off his melancholy mood. "Just hoping the next call is anything but OB."

"Why?" He'd mentioned that before, but she didn't understand. "You must have OB emergencies show up in the ER all the time."

He grimaced and nodded. "Yeah, but there's always other docs around, and an OB provider who is always in house and willing to come down at a moment's notice to take over. Being up in the air like that . . ." He shrugged and shook his head. "Terrifying."

She sensed there was more to the story. "Does your aversion to OB emergencies have anything to do with why you avoid discussing Christmas?"

He shot her a surprised look. "Um, maybe."

More secrets. He'd told her about the email from the woman claiming to be his birth mother, but clearly he wasn't willing to tell her anything more.

"Listen, I know you're a private kind of guy, but I'm happy to listen if you need to confide in someone. I hope you know I won't blab about your personal life, Drake."

"I never thought you would." He hesitated, then added, "It's a long story."

"I'm willing to listen," she repeated. "It doesn't have to be here, where we can be interrupted at the drop of a hat, but whenever. You were there to help me get through the flu, I'd like to return the favor."

The corner of his mouth tipped up in a half smile. "Okay, maybe after work, then. You might be right about talking about it."

"I'd like that." She was humbled at his decision to place his trust in her. "Tonight works, or another day. You let me know."

"Tonight," he said in a rueful tone. "Otherwise, I might talk myself out of it."

That made her laugh. "Tonight works great." She tried to think of what kind of food she had in the house to offer. Not much other than cheese, crackers, and soup. "I'd offer to cook, but I'm afraid there isn't much to make unless you like grilled cheese and chicken noodle or tomato soup. That's pretty much all I bought at the store last week."

"How about I bring dinner? Chinese takeout? Or roasted chicken?"

"Roasted chicken would be great." She put her hand on the upper portion of her stomach. "The pizza is already giving me heartburn."

"Roasted chicken it is." He glanced down at her abdomen, then quickly looked away. "Sorry about the heartburn."

"Hey, I'll take heartburn over throwing up any day." She waved her hand. "Not sure why, but I'm feeling better in that department."

"Maybe you're farther along than you originally thought?"

It felt odd to be discussing her pregnancy with Drake, especially since she still hadn't heard a word from Cal, the baby's father. "No, I'm fairly certain I have the dates correct. I'm sure my OB will validate that."

"Ultrasounds are very commonly used to estimate gestational age," Drake agreed. "I'm sure your doctor will schedule one soon."

"I can't wait, although I'm torn between keeping the baby's gender a secret or finding out ahead of time."

"We—" He stopped abruptly.

Before she could ask we—what their pagers went off.

This time, she had no qualms about flying or landing.

Maybe because she was glad their shift was going by quickly.

She was looking forward to seeing Drake after work.

DRAKE COULDN'T BELIEVE he'd almost blurted the truth about how he and Serena had decided to wait to find out the baby's gender. Because they'd wanted it to be a surprise.

He hadn't known he had a son until the infant had been stillborn. Drake's heart still ached from the loss.

But there was no denying his interest in the pretty blonde pilot.

They had a date. Tonight. To share dinner. What was he thinking?

That he was tired of being alone.

The stark truth was as simple and complicated as that. He was tired of being alone, but getting involved with another woman? One that was pregnant? There were plenty of other women he worked with. Not necessarily at Lifeline, but at the hospital.

Too bad he wasn't interested in any of them. Even now, thinking back, he remembered a couple of women who'd asked him out. He'd turned them down, nowhere near ready to hit the social scene, but at the moment he couldn't even remember who they were much less what they'd looked like.

The only explanation was that he'd lost his mind.

He focused on the transfer, a young man who'd been in a bad snowmobile accident up in Rhinelander and needed to be transported down to Trinity Medical Center. Not an OB call, thankfully.

He shouldn't have been surprised, Megan was astute

enough to pick up on his aversion to OB calls and to celebrating Christmas. He wished now that he hadn't promised to
talk about his past. He'd rather look forward to spending time
with Megan without slogging through his personal baggage.

After he and Ivan boarded the chopper, he listened as
Megan spoke with the paramedic base about their call. He
hadn't realized the flight between Milwaukee and
Rhinelander would take a little over an hour one way.

A glance at his watch confirmed they should be back a
few minutes before the end of their shift. If they didn't run
into any problems.

Not his usual MO while responding to calls, however.
Hopefully, this one would prove uneventful.

They were in the air almost twenty minutes when the
call came in from the paramedic base.

"Lifeline, your call to Rhinelander has been canceled.
Repeat, your call has been canceled."

"Ten-four," Megan responded. "Turning around to
return to Lifeline."

The chopper made a wide one-eighty-degree turn in the
air, before resuming its course. Drake cued his mic. "Base,
this is Dr. Thorton. Can you tell me why the transfer has
been canceled?"

"We were informed the patient passed away."

He didn't move for a long moment. Ivan sighed heavily
and shook his head. "That's not good."

"No, it's not. Thanks for the update." He clicked off from
the call.

It was a long silent trip back to the hangar. He wondered
how Jared would feel about the waste of fuel in responding
to a call that was ultimately canceled.

The last hour of their shift was uneventful. No additional calls came in. The night shift arrived bringing Holt Baxter and Kristin Page as the physician and nurse on duty, and Reese was the pilot.

The hand-off didn't take long. Kristin and Holt discussed doing follow-up visits since there were no calls waiting in the wings.

"If you do, would you check in on Infant Male Browning? I transferred him to the NICU at Children's Memorial Hospital a few days ago. I'd like to know how he's doing."

"We can do that," Kristin agreed.

"Thanks." He wouldn't mind hearing about all the patients he'd cared for, but the little preemie held a special place in his heart. He prayed the little guy was doing better. That he'd find a way to survive and thrive when his own son hadn't.

When it was time to leave, he walked Megan to her car. "Give me about twenty minutes to get home, change, and then pick up the food."

"Okay." She glanced up at him from beneath her lashes. "Do you live far from here?"

"I have a condo in The Hill."

She raised a brow. "Very nice."

He shrugged. "It's okay, nothing fancy." He kept his hands tucked into his pockets while she opened her car door and slid in behind the wheel.

"Twenty minutes," he repeated.

"See you then." She shut the door and started the engine.

He hurried through a quick shower, changed into jeans and a sweater, then stopped at the grocery store for a rotisserie chicken. He added mashed potatoes and gravy, along with steamed broccoli. He should have asked what kinds of veggies she liked but figured if she wasn't a fan, he'd finish the broccoli himself.

He made it to her apartment with two minutes to spare. This time, there was no one coming out to provide him a way to get inside, so he had to buzz the intercom.

"Come in," Megan said.

His pulse kicked up a notch as he entered the building and took the stairs to her second-floor apartment. His first visit had been to help out a sick friend.

This was something more.

He rapped on the door. She opened it, looking amazingly lovely with her blond hair loose around her face. She was dressed much like he was, in comfy blue jeans and a pale blue sweater that made her eyes stand out.

His mouth went desert dry, and it took a minute for him to jump-start his brain cells. "Hey, you look great. I hope you're hungry."

"Surprisingly, I am." She opened the door wider to give him room to come in. "I'm not sure if this not-feeling-sick thing is good, I'm liable to pack on the pounds by eating everything in sight."

"I don't think you have anything to worry about." In truth, he liked her curves. What was the point of being stick thin? As he carried the bag of food to the table, he'd noticed she had it set for two, with a lit candle in the center.

It was a romantic gesture and a wordless acknowledgment that their relationship had turned a corner from friendship to a date.

A flutter of panic hit hard. He tried to ignore it.

"Broccoli! My favorite!"

He smiled. "Mine too."

Within minutes they were sitting across from each other

eating the delicious chicken, potatoes, and broccoli. "Having that last call canceled was disappointing," Megan said.

"Yeah. How does Jared deal with that kind of thing? It's a waste of fuel at the very least."

Megan nodded. "It is, but it's part of the business. I think deaths that occur during our transfers are viewed as far worse."

"I get that."

There was a moment of silence, but he didn't find it uncomfortable, the way it sometimes was with people you didn't know very well. Odd how close he felt to Megan.

She didn't ask anything personal until they'd finished their meal. She waved away his offer to help with the dishes and asked him to sit in the living room for a few minutes.

When she had the table cleared and the leftover food put away, she joined him.

"You lost someone close to you," she said softly.

"Yes." He forced himself to meet her gaze. "My wife and infant son."

She sucked in a harsh breath and took his hand in hers. "Oh, Drake. How terrible for you. To lose your wife and son at Christmas must have been incredibly difficult."

He nodded because he couldn't speak. His throat had closed up to the point he could barely breathe.

"My heart goes out to you." Megan lifted his hand and gently kissed it.

It was the sweetest embrace he'd been given over the past year. He found himself wrapping his arm around her shoulders and bringing her close.

For several minutes she didn't speak but simply rested her head in the crook of his shoulder. Then she pulled away, just enough to look into his eyes.

"I know it isn't easy to understand God's plan, but I hope you know he has something special in store for you."

Again, his throat tightened, making it impossible for him to respond. Words wouldn't come, so he put his feelings into words by simply lifting her chin and gently kissing her.

The way he'd longed to do for the past week.

9

M egan melted into Drake's embrace, savoring his kiss. Warning signals were flashing in the back of her brain, but she ignored them.

Drake's kiss made her feel beautiful and desired in a way she hadn't felt in what seemed like forever. It made a mockery of what she'd experienced with Cal, but this wasn't the time for self-recrimination.

From this moment, she wanted nothing more than to look forward toward the future.

Their kiss ended when they both needed to breathe. Drake rested his forehead against hers. "Wow," he whispered.

She smiled. "Yeah, wow."

He lifted his head and looked down at her. Slowly, the joy in his eyes faded. "Listen, Megan, I care about you . . ."

She grimaced and pushed away, rising to her feet. "Don't. It was just a kiss, Drake. No reason to make such a big deal out of it."

He reached up to snag her hand, preventing her from walking away. "It was more than just a kiss to me. Which is why I feel the need to warn you. The anniversary of my wife and son's death is two days from now. I am not sure I'm emotionally ready to jump into another relationship."

Her flash of anger faded. "I don't remember saying anything about a relationship. It's not like this is a good time for me either. I'm pregnant and should be focused on my baby not kissing a handsome doc."

"Handsome?" He flashed a crooked smile. "Thanks."

She rolled her eyes. "Seriously? I can't be the first woman to point that out."

"I haven't even thought about being with another woman until you." His gaze turned serious. "But as much as I'm tempted, I don't think I can commit to anything right now."

"I understand. And I appreciate your honesty." Something Cal certainly hadn't given her. She ignored the searing disappointment and forced a smile. "I don't blame you for backing off, especially considering the fact that I'm pregnant outside of being married." The words were difficult to push past her throat. So far no one had passed judgment on her, but she suspected it was only a matter of time.

And while she knew giving herself to Cal was wrong, she couldn't regret the fact that she was carrying a child. A child that she already loved, even though it was clear that Cal didn't.

"It's not about that at all," Drake swiftly denied. He let go of her hand and raked his fingers through his dark hair. "I—just need to get through the next few weeks. Maybe once all this Christmas stuff is over, I'll feel better."

"Oh, Drake. Christmas is supposed to be a time of love, of blessings, of new beginnings. Not something to get through as quickly as possible."

"Yeah, well unfortunately I don't feel any of those things

about the Christmas holiday." His expression turned grim. "For me it's a reminder of everything I loved and lost."

Her heart ached for him, but she didn't know what to say or what to do to help him get through this. She tried to imagine how she would feel if she lost her baby and a husband on the same day right before Christmas. Would she turn her back on celebrating the Birth of Jesus? She didn't think so, but maybe. It was hard to imagine the magnitude of his loss.

"Way to kill the mood, huh?" He sighed. "I'd better go." Drake rose to his feet and edged toward the door. "Thanks for sharing dinner with me."

"Thanks for buying dinner." She followed him, regretting the loss of the easy camaraderie between them.

He didn't touch her again but simply smiled and tucked his hands into his pockets. "Good night, Megan. See you at work."

"Good night, Drake." She watched him walk away, then closed and locked her apartment door.

She worked the following day but knew Drake had off because of working over the weekend. It was a bit scary to realize how much she wanted to work with him.

To see him. To spend more time with him. Not just at work, but alone like this, sharing a cozy romantic meal.

She put her hand over her stomach and slowly shook her head. Her emotions were already tangled in a knot over Drake Thorton, and they'd experienced exactly one date and one heated kiss.

Would she even see him again by January when his Lifeline rotation was over?

If not, she needed to put an end to this right now.

Before she lost her heart to another man who was equally determined to walk away.

On Wednesday, her day off, Megan decided to do a little shopping for maternity clothes. She had to remember to ask Jared about where she could find the two-piece pregnancy flight suits Shelly had made.

She decided to go to actual stores that sold maternity clothes rather than shopping online. Clothes were always tricky for her to buy without trying on, she was short and curvy, so some styles fit well and others didn't. And she was looking at becoming even more curvy as the weeks passed.

The weather had turned bitter cold. Still, she wrapped a scarf around her neck, pulled on a matching slate blue hat and gloves, and braved the elements.

There were many designs to choose from, although she was a bit shell-shocked at the prices. Why would adding an elastic panel to a pair of jeans make them cost so much more than regular ones? Especially when they didn't need the added cost of a zipper? It was crazy.

Being mindful of her budget, considering she had no idea how long she'd be allowed to fly in her condition, she only purchased a couple of maternity tops and one pair of jeans. The amount was still more than she'd really wanted to spend, but she decided it was a start.

Her stomach was growling by the time she finished shopping, so she stopped by the deli near Lifeline on her way back to her apartment. Her morning sickness wasn't nearly as bad as it had been, so she decided to take a chance and go with a French dip roast beef sandwich.

She turned and raked her gaze over the crowd to find a table. She saw Drake seated at a table by himself. His gaze locked with hers for a long moment before he lifted a hand and waved her over.

Warily, she carried her tray over to join him, her shopping bag banging against her hip. He gestured to it. "I see you've been shopping at Gloria's Maternity."

"Yes, figured I needed to because my jeans are fitting a bit too snuggly." She dropped into the chair across from him. "I didn't expect to find you here."

"I'm grabbing a quick bite to eat before going in to work the other half of Matt's shift to cover for him as he's got the flu."

"Ugh, poor guy. I know all too well how that feels." She glanced up at the server who brought over her French dip sandwich. "Thanks."

"Yeah, although he doesn't seem as bad as you were." Drake eyed her curiously over his burger. "I'm sure your morning sickness didn't help."

"Probably not." She gave a quick smile, then dug into her meal. "Yum. This is good."

His lopsided smile tugged at her heart. "I bet it's nice to eat something besides saltine crackers with cheese."

"For sure." She took another bite. "I forgot to ask you this last night, but have you decided to reach out to the woman who might be your birth mother?"

He didn't answer right away, and she wondered if he might change the subject to avoid discussing it. But then he slowly nodded. "I almost responded to her this morning, but then I got the call from Matt about working today, so I didn't. But yeah, I'm thinking about it."

"She doesn't know you're a doctor, right? So this wouldn't be about money."

He grimaced. "Sad to say, but that is something I considered. I didn't put it in my profile information, but anyone can google me and find out I'm enrolled in an emergency medicine residency program. Thanks to social media, that isn't much of a secret."

"I guess you're right, nothing is secret anymore these days." Which only made her think about Cal and Emily, who likely had photos of themselves together on various social media platforms.

"I'll respond to her message tonight," Drake said, interrupting her thoughts. "She mentioned wanting to meet with me, she lives in the Racine area."

"Meeting in person is a big step." She looked at him curiously. "Interesting that she doesn't live far from Milwaukee. Is this where you grew up?"

He nodded. "My parents adopted me as a way to save their failing marriage, which of course didn't work. I was about five when they divorced, and I grew up being bounced back and forth between parents. My dad and his new wife live in The Hill, and my mom and her husband live in Burlington. I don't really see much of either one of them anymore."

"Why on earth not?" She didn't hide her shock. "You're still their son."

He shrugged, but she could tell the wounds inflicted by parents who tried to use him as a way to save their floundering marriage were deeply embedded. "Not really. Most parents fight over who gets custody of a child, but mine argued about who had to take me."

"Oh, Drake." She couldn't stand the idea of parents fighting over who had to take him. "That's just awful."

"Yeah, well, I'm not saying adoption is bad, because it's the best alternative for most kids. Just not for me."

Because his parents had adopted him for the wrong reasons. "Do you have half brothers and sisters?"

"Yeah, a couple of each. They were okay with me

growing up, but over time, being included in family gatherings grew less and less." He finished his burger, then took care of his trash. "Sorry, but I have to run. Matt is waiting for me."

"I understand. Have a good shift." She wanted nothing more than to give him a big hug, but she remained seated as he left the deli.

She couldn't believe Drake had such a horrible experience growing up. The fact that he was able to graduate high school and college and medical school was astounding. After beating all the adversity in his life, he met and married his wife, planned a family, only to lose it all just before Christmas.

No wonder he was extremely quiet, serious, and subdued.

Frankly, if she were in his shoes? She wasn't sure she'd get out of bed every morning.

The fact that he'd accomplished so much more was humbling.

DRAKE SPENT his shift wondering what on earth possessed him to unload on Megan's slim shoulders about his past.

For someone who'd thrived on keeping his emotional issues private, he'd become a big blabbermouth.

The afternoon dragged by slowly. They had one trauma call for a single car crash into a tree, the driver had several fractures but overall remained stable on the short flight to Trinity Medical Center. When that call was finished, Jenna Reed, the paramedic on duty, went back to doing her homework for her nursing program, leaving him staring at the email from the woman claiming to be his birth mother.

Jolene Nevin.

Once he'd read her message, he hadn't been able to get her name out of his head. Had she named him Drake? Or had that been a name given to him by his adopted parents? And what difference did it make? He wasn't getting rid of his name. Despite his conflicted childhood, he didn't want to give up the little bit of identity he had.

They didn't get another call until near the end of their shift. Another trauma call, this one from a snowmobile accident at Pike Lake. The lake hadn't been all the way frozen over, and a snowmobiler had gone down through the ice. Other snowmobilers had pulled the guy out of the water, but their patient Benny Cooper needed to get to Trinity ASAP.

Pike Lake wasn't far, but Dirk landed far from the lake so as not to cause issues with the force of the chopper blades breaking up the ice. The rescue team members were working on Benny as they brought him up to shore.

"Any idea what his core temp is?" Drake asked as Jenna began connecting the snowmobiler to their equipment.

"No clue," the paramedic said. "We haven't gained much ground in performing CPR, so I'm sure it's bad."

Drake nodded and took over doing chest compressions once he and Jenna had transferred Benny onto their Lifeline gurney.

"You need to stop for a moment so we can get him to the chopper." Jenna gently pushed him off the guy's chest and began to push the gurney over the bumpy ground. He added his strength so they were practically running back to the helicopter.

Once they had Benny inside the chopper, he resumed his chest compressions, leaving Jenna the task of doing all the documenting. She made him stop CPR again, long enough to wrap Benny in a heating blanket.

"I'll take over in five minutes," she said as he resumed doing chest compressions.

He nodded to indicate he heard and understood. He was stronger than Jenna but knew the importance of doing frequent handoffs to keep the compressions going strong and deep.

Despite the nearly zero temperatures outside, he worked up a sweat. After the designated five minutes, they traded roles as Dirk quickly flew them to Trinity.

He requested a hot unload, then took over doing chest compressions until Dirk had them down on the landing pad.

"Take over, I'll go out and grab him from the back." He didn't wait for Jenna's response, but jumped out of the chopper and ran around to the back hatch.

From there, they couldn't do any more CPR until they had him inside the building. Jenna being the smallest of them, jumped on the edge of the gurney to continue doing compressions as he and the ER docs wheeled Benny into the elevators and down to the trauma bay.

The rest of the trauma team quickly took over. Benny still didn't have a pulse, so they continued doing CPR while they ran some labs and put in a central line.

He and Jenna backed off, giving the trauma team room to work. Soon enough, he'd be on the other side, receiving patients from ambulances and helicopters rather than bringing them in. He was enjoying his Lifeline rotation yet looked forward to being back in the relatively calm and stable environment of the emergency department.

"We'd better go, our shift is almost over." Jenna's voice pulled him from his thoughts.

"Yeah, okay." After using the hospital bleach wipes to clean up their equipment, they returned to where Dirk waited in the chopper.

The night shift crew was waiting for them in the debriefing room when they arrived. Nate was the pilot on duty and Holt Baxter the physician, working again with his new fiancée Kristin Page.

"I heard Benny Cooper was just brought in," Holt said solemnly.

Drake exchanged surprised glances with Jenna. "You know him?"

"He's the owner of Coopers on the Lake, a really nice restaurant." Holt shrugged. "There are dozens of posts already on social media about how he went under the ice."

Of course there was. This was the era of instant messaging and gratification. "He's in rough shape," Drake admitted. "By the time we reached the ER, his core temp was still barely ninety-three point six degrees Fahrenheit."

Holt let out a low whistle. "Doesn't sound like he's going to make it."

"Unfortunately, I agree. We did CPR on him the entire flight, without much success," Jenna said with a sigh.

"I'm sure you did your best." Holt glanced at Kristin. "Let's check in later as a follow-up visit. Maybe being hypothermic worked in his favor."

"Okay," Kristin agreed.

"Speaking of follow-up visits, what did you find out about Infant Male Browning?" Drake glanced from Holt to Kristin.

"He's doing okay, not out of the woods, but certainly not worse. They're cautiously optimistic." Kristin used her fingers to make air quotes around the last two words.

A small flicker of hope in the area of his heart grew brighter. "Really? I'd like to see him for myself."

"You can go now," Jenna offered. "We're finished for the day."

He hesitated, then nodded. Why not go check on the little guy he'd helped keep alive during the transfer from Sheboygan to Children's Memorial? "Okay, I'll see you tomorrow, Jenna."

"Oh, you're covering for Matt again?" she asked.

"Yeah, no sense in having him pass along more germs." He drew on his Lifeline jacket and headed out into the frigid cold temperatures.

Ducking his head against the wind, he walked over to Children's Memorial Hospital. He took the elevators to the NICU, then had to buzz the front desk to gain entrance to the unit.

"Can I help you?" One of the NICU nurses stopped and looked at him curiously.

He pulled out his Lifeline ID badge. "I'm Dr. Thorton from Lifeline, doing a follow-up visit on Infant Male Browning. He was transferred from Sheboygan Memorial a couple of days ago."

"Oh yes, they're actually calling him Jonah Browning. He's right over here." She led the way over to an isolette at the end of the row.

He recognized the little guy right away. For a long moment he stood staring down at him, amazed that his heart rate was doing much better at 140 beats per minute.

Jonah suddenly began to cry, making him smile. The kid had a healthy set of lungs on him, that was for sure. And he was big, at least compared to most of the preemies in isolettes nearby.

God has a plan for you.

Megan's words came back to him, and he put his hand against the glass of the isolette. Was this part of God's plan? To send him in a helicopter to save this little boy?

Maybe. As much as the loss of Serena and Lance had left a hole in his heart, he suddenly understood he hadn't died with them.

Megan and Kate were right. Where there was life, there was hope.

10

W hen Megan entered the debriefing room the following morning, she was surprised to find it empty. Usually the pilot sat by the radar screen to keep up on the weather. Following the sounds of laughter, she headed into the lounge.

Kristin Page, Holt Baxter, and Nate were decorating a lopsided Christmas tree set up in the corner of the room. But instead of using traditional holiday ornaments, they were using Lifeline supplies. Seeing the way they'd hung IV catheters, urinary catheters, and dressings on the various branches made her smile.

"That's the saddest Christmas tree I've ever seen," she said with a shake of her head. "Ingenious, but sad. You couldn't find any real Christmas items to use? And what are you going to use for the star on top?"

Kristin flashed a grin. "We were thinking of using an emesis basin but can't get it to sit right."

"I think this bedpan might work." Holt held it up, then lightly balanced it on the top of the tree. "See?"

She wrinkled her nose. "Gross."

"The supplies are clean, and mostly outdated, so we're not wasting them," Holt offered. The bedpan slid down and landed on the floor with a thud. Holt picked it up and placed it back on top of the tree, jamming the top of the tree into the opening.

"Pretty sure bedpans don't expire," Kristin pointed out dryly.

"When's the last time we used one in a flight?" Holt spread his hands wide. "Some of this stuff has been gathering dust since the eighties."

Megan lifted a brow. "Lifeline has been around for that long?"

"Yes, since 1984." When they all stared at Holt, he shook his head in disgust. "What? I can't help the way my brain files useless facts away for future reference."

"Oh yeah, your brain is a file cabinet all right." Kristin lightly tapped her fingertip on his temple, then went up on her tiptoes to peer into his ear. "Yep. I can see those drawers opening and closing as we speak."

"You mock me, but you know it's true." Holt swung her in for a quick hug and kiss.

The easy camaraderie between the newly engaged couple, Kristin and Holt, was something she secretly envied. And more proof that what she and Cal shared wasn't even close to real love and caring. Cal hadn't displayed a great sense of humor and tended to become cranky and irritable when things didn't go his way.

Enough. Thinking about Cal was counterproductive. Especially since he still hadn't acknowledged her messages about her pregnancy.

"What is that?" Drake's voice had her turning to face him. She hadn't realized he'd be working today. But then she remembered Drake was covering for Matt Abbott who had the flu.

"You don't recognize a Christmas tree when you see one?" Kristin teased. "Where's your sense of humor?"

Megan moved closer to Drake in a silent show of support. She knew the reason he avoided the holiday, but the others didn't. She kept her tone light and teasing. "The bedpan on top was Holt's idea."

After a long second, the corner of Drake's mouth curved up in a smile. "Pretty pathetic, don't you think?"

"We work with what we have," Kristin said, waving an impatient hand. "And what we have isn't much."

"I hope Jared doesn't mind the way you wasted our supplies," Drake said.

"Most of them are outdated or rarely used." Holt took a step back and nodded his approval. "Besides, it's a good way to get into the holiday spirit."

"Bah humbug," Drake deadpanned.

"If the tree is finished, we should get down to business," Nate said, moving toward the debriefing room. "Who are we waiting for?"

"I'm here," Ivan said, coming through the doorway bringing in a cold gust of winter air. "Overslept this morning."

"Is Bethany all right?" Megan asked.

"She has the flu." Ivan plopped into a chair. "She woke up about two in the morning and didn't fall back asleep until almost four. I managed to get a total of five hours of sleep. But at least my wife has the day off, otherwise we'd be scrambling for childcare."

Megan nodded, her chest tight. She wouldn't have the option of a partner taking the day off to stay home with a sick kid. Her parents were gone, both having passed away from cancer, and she didn't have brothers or sisters.

The responsibility of being a single parent was suddenly overwhelming.

There was no point in worrying about that now. She hadn't even had her first doctor's appointment. Hadn't felt the baby move, which according to the books she'd read would start at about sixteen weeks.

"Any pending transfers?" Drake asked when everyone took a seat in the debriefing room.

"Nope. It was a quiet night," Holt said. "We only did two calls, both without incident."

"Okay, then what about the weather conditions?" Drake's gaze shifted to Nate and Megan. "Anything to worry about there?"

"Cloudy skies, but not a lot of wind," Nate said with a shrug. "Nothing to worry about from my perspective."

Megan glanced at the radar, taking in the wind pattern and cloud cover. "I agree, we're good to fly."

Drake nodded but didn't say anything more. Holt and Kristin left, as did Nate. Ivan disappeared into the lounge and stretched out on the sofa. She couldn't blame him for trying to get a little sleep.

"Have you heard how Matt is doing?"

Drake shook his head. "No, but he told me he'd call later to let me know how it's going. If he's better, he may pick up one of my shifts."

"Sounds reasonable." She wanted to sigh at the fact that they were talking about work or the weather. "Have you responded to your birth mother yet?"

"Yeah, I sent her a message last night." Drake pulled his phone out of his pocket and thumbed open his email. "No response yet."

"I'm impressed." She tipped her head, regarding him thoughtfully. "What made you decide to respond?"

He shrugged. "I went to see Jonah Browning last night. He's doing much better."

"Jonah Browning? Oh, the preemie we transported from Sheboygan." She found it difficult to keep all the names of their patients straight.

"Yeah. I guess I thought that if Jonah can survive against the odds, then I should at least meet this woman who thinks she's my birth mother."

"Yes, you should," she agreed. "It can't hurt."

He lifted a brow. "Says the woman who isn't adopted."

She grimaced. "You're right. It's easy for me to say. But you went onto the website for a reason, so deep down, you must be curious."

He shook his head. "Originally, I wanted medical history information for the sake of my baby. Now, I'm not sure what I want."

She believed he wanted a family but didn't say the words out loud.

"I need more coffee." Drake stood and headed into the lounge.

After sitting quietly for a moment, savoring the lack of morning sickness, she pulled out her phone. Maybe she wasn't giving Cal enough credit. Maybe he would want to be part of their child's life. She found Cal's social media page, thinking maybe she'd drop him a note there.

But the photo that stared back at her wasn't Cal alone, it was Cal with a beautiful dark-haired woman.

And beneath the image were the words: *She said yes!*

Said yes to what? Marrying him? Mere months after he broke off his engagement with her?

She stared at the photo for a long time. The date stamp

indicated the photo was put up yesterday. Which meant he had access to a phone and/or computer.

But he still hadn't responded to her messages about their baby.

She set her phone down. Drawing in a deep breath, then letting it out in a long whoosh.

Okay then. Apparently, she was raising this child entirely on her own.

~

DRAKE NEEDED something to distract him from looking at his email every five seconds.

The bedpan topping the Christmas tree had him shaking his head in bemusement. He couldn't deny the cheery lights brightened the mood even if the so-called ornaments left a lot to be desired. They consisted of tools they used to save people's lives, but he still wondered what Jared would say when he saw it.

Ivan looked as if he might be sleeping, so he didn't wake him. He prowled restlessly around the room, fighting the urge to check his email.

The downtime between calls was the most difficult part of the job for him to handle. There was the occasional day that the ER wasn't insanely busy, but not like this. He considered sitting at the computer to study for his boards that he'd have to take come the end of June, but he couldn't drudge up any interest.

June was a good six months away. And he'd already had a lot of interesting real-life experiences that would help him when the time came.

He forced himself to pull up the practice exam on the

computer. After a couple of questions, his mind began to wander.

What if Jolene Nevin wanted to set up a meeting? Would he go? And what kind of proof might she have to prove she's his birth mother? Sure, they could have a DNA test done, but that would take time and money.

He couldn't deny being curious about the circumstances of her giving him up for adoption. Mostly likely she'd been a teenager without much family support. It made him think of Megan and the way she'd gone pale at hearing about Ivan's daughter waking up with the flu.

Who would be there to help Megan when her baby was sick? Not that jerk of a father, that's for sure.

He answered a few more questions before his pager went off in tandem with Ivan's. The paramedic groaned and rolled up into a sitting position.

"Trauma call, car vs semitruck," Drake read the page out loud. "Two adults, a man and woman, female is about eight months pregnant."

"Let's go," Ivan said, rising to his feet and reaching for their bag of supplies.

Eight months pregnant. The words were lit up like neon in his brain. Why was he getting all the OB calls?

Technically, this was Matt's shift, so it wouldn't normally have been his call. But he'd be the one to respond.

Megan already had the chopper pulled out of the hangar. She held a clipboard in her hand and was doing a quick last-minute check.

She glanced at him, her clear gray eyes shadowed with concern. He tried to smile reassuringly.

What choice did he have other than to do his best while praying both the mother and baby survived?

"Ready?" Megan asked, reaching for the door to the pilot's seat.

"Yes." He gave her a nod and followed Ivan into the back of the chopper. Within minutes, Megan had the engines fired up and the blades whirling. He listened as she was given permission to take off and kept his gaze out the window as she banked the chopper around and toward the interstate.

"Man, I don't feel good," Ivan muttered.

He pierced him with a look. "What do you mean?"

Ivan grimaced and pressed his hand to his gut. "I feel sick."

"The flu?" Drake tried not to panic. "Are you going to be okay to help with this call?"

Ivan nodded, but he could tell the paramedic was fighting the urge to throw up.

"Stay with me," he encouraged as Megan closed the distance to the scene of the crash. "Once we return to Lifeline, we'll find someone to cover your shift."

"Okay." Ivan's tone was weak, and Drake wondered just how much help the paramedic would be.

Enough, hopefully, to get the worst of the two patients transported to Trinity Medical Center.

Megan landed the chopper on a vacant stretch of the freeway. He jumped out and went around to open the back hatch for the gurney. Ivan followed more slowly, clearly not feeling well.

"Sorry," Ivan muttered. He abruptly veered off and threw up along the side of the road.

Drake knew there was nothing he could do but grab the bag of supplies from Ivan and continue on to check the status of their patients. The paramedics looked relieved to see him.

"This is Susan O'Malley, and she's in labor."

"How far apart are the contractions?" He set the duffel bag down and crouched in front of the woman. Susan was in the back seat of the car. The front was crushed in like an accordion. No blood on his patient, which was reassuring.

"Three minutes," she said between panting breaths. She looked at him with wide pleading brown eyes. "Make them stop. It's too soon. I'm not due for six weeks."

Drake battled a wave of panic. "Okay, listen, you need to stay calm, okay? We're going to take good care of you." He glanced at the paramedic closest to him. "Where's the driver?"

"On his way to Trinity. He had some chest pain but no EKG changes, so we decided to take him via ambulance. We thought it would be better to have this patient in the chopper."

Better to deliver a baby thousands of feet in the air? Not even close.

"My partner has the flu, I think you're going to need to take her via ambulance." Drake hoped Jared would support his decision.

"Ohhh, I feel like I have to push." Susan's voice had risen with alarm.

What? Push? Sweat popped out on his forehead. This couldn't be happening. Could it? His mouth was desert dry, but he tried to keep his expression from showing his feelings. "Okay, I'm going to take a look, see how dilated you are."

After drawing on a pair of gloves, he bent her legs at the knees and carefully removed her undergarments. When he saw the baby's head crowning, he knew this was it.

He was going to end up delivering this baby right here, right now.

Please, Lord, please give me the strength to save this child's life.

"Oh boy," the paramedic muttered under his breath.

"Or girl," Drake said to lighten things up. "Get me some towels and sheets to put under her. Have either of you delivered a baby before?"

"I did once," the paramedic to his right said. "But that was a long time ago."

Drake had also assisted with giving birth while on his OB rotation, which had also been over a year ago. "Glove up and help me. I also want blankets to wrap the baby in once it's born."

"I'll get them," the other paramedic, the one who didn't have experience delivering babies, said.

"It's coming," Susan said between pants. "And it hurts!"

"Yes, the baby is coming, you're doing a great job, Susan. It's not going to hurt for long." Drake put one hand on her abdomen to feel for the next contraction, while supporting the baby's head with the other. "Okay, next contraction you're going to push really hard."

"Ohhh," Susan let out a wail, but then pushed hard when the contraction hit. He felt the baby slide forward and used both hands to gently turn the baby's head as it emerged from the birth canal.

"Good, you're doing great, Susan. The baby's head is out, one more push and your son or daughter will be born." He met Susan's gaze. "One more big push."

She groaned and pushed again. He eased the infant's shoulders out, then caught the baby in both hands. The paramedic handed him the blanket, and he wiped the mucus away from the baby's nose and mouth. For several long seconds, the infant didn't move. Didn't breathe.

His chest went tight with fear. No! This couldn't be happening. *The baby couldn't be stillborn!*

His training kicked in, and he flicked the bottom of the baby's feet, then gently stimulated the infant's chest. Instantly, the little girl began to cry.

The relief was staggering. The baby was alive! And so was the mother.

He clamped the umbilical cord and brought the wrapped bundle up and placed the baby in her mother's arms. "You have a beautiful baby girl."

"Amanda." Susan's eyes filled with tears as she cuddled the baby close. "We've named her Amanda."

"That's a beautiful name." Drake felt himself getting choked up. The image of his stillborn son flashed in his mind, but he shoved it away.

Lance was gone, but Amanda wasn't. She was still crying, but he didn't mind the noise.

The sound of life.

"Shouldn't we do Apgar or something?" the paramedic asked.

"Yeah, I'm calling it a six and a ten." The score given to a baby at birth was a way to judge how well they were doing. Considering the baby didn't breathe right away, he lowered the first score, but frankly, out here in the middle of the freeway, the numbers didn't much matter.

The fact that both mom and baby were fine did.

He rose to his feet. "I think you guys can take her from here. No need to travel via helicopter now."

"Yeah, sure." The two paramedics looked at each other. "Thanks for the help, Doc."

"You're welcome." Drake backed away, taking the gurney with him. When he turned, Megan was standing there, her eyes bright against her pale skin.

"That was—incredible and scary at the same time." Her voice came out in a hoarse whisper.

"The mother and baby are both fine." He hadn't realized she was there but realized she must have been about to offer her help. "Where's Ivan?"

"Uh, back there, somewhere." She still looked pale and shaken. "He's sick."

"Okay, we need get back to the hangar. Ivan is in no condition to fly."

Megan nodded but didn't move. Instead, she stood for a long moment, her hand pressed against her lower abdomen as if imagining the moment her own baby would be born.

Drake found himself eager to support her when that day came.

If she wanted him to.

11

Watching Drake delivering a baby had hit hard. Not just the reality of giving birth, which was incredible and scary enough, but the way Drake had been so calm and cool under pressure.

Come next June, it would be her turn. The realization was sobering.

She didn't know much about being a mother. Had barely gotten used to the concept of being pregnant, much less anything else. Imagining what her life would be like beyond the next few months was impossible.

Pulling herself together, she fell into step beside Drake as they returned to the chopper. Ivan was there, leaning weakly against the bird. He offered a pathetic smile. "Sorry."

"It's no problem," Drake said, waving a hand. "We need to get you back to the hangar."

Megan jumped up into the pilot's seat, waiting for the two men to get themselves secured in the back. After requesting permission from the paramedic base, she lifted the chopper off the ground.

The trip back to Lifeline didn't take long. Ivan was the

first one off the helicopter, rushing inside the building as if the devil himself was hot on his heels.

She knew exactly how he felt, having made the same trip not long ago.

"We're grounded until I can get someone in to cover Ivan's shift," Drake said as they walked into the hangar. "I might even have to drive him home."

"I can do it," she offered.

"No, you should stay here with the helicopter. Hopefully, the ride won't take long."

"I'll make the calls for his replacement, then."

"Thanks."

The next hour dragged by slowly. She made phone calls for help in covering Ivan's shift as Drake drove Ivan home. Jenna Reed promised to be there within the hour. When Drake returned, she filled him in.

"Glad to hear it." Drake washed his hands at the sink. "I hope I don't catch that nasty bug. I had to pull over for Ivan twice on the way home."

"I feel bad for his wife, having a sick baby and a sick husband to take care of."

"True." Drake dried his hands and dropped into the chair beside her. "Are you okay?"

"Me? Fine. Childbirth is amazing."

"And scary."

She grimaced and nodded. "Yeah. But I have faith in God that everything will work out."

"Good."

She glanced around, verifying they were still alone. "Have you heard from your birth mother?"

"Been too busy to look." Drake reluctantly pulled out his cell phone. He swiped at the screen, then lifted his gaze to hers. "She responded. Wants to meet for coffee."

"That's great." She was glad he'd taken this first step. "When?"

"Tomorrow at noon." He cleared his throat. "I mentioned to her that I have the day off."

"I'm glad. I hope she has the answers you're looking for."

There was a brief pause. "Megan, I know you have the day off too. Will you please come with me?"

Her pulse leaped in her chest. "Are you sure?"

"I don't want to do this alone." He glanced at her sheepishly. "I'm not sure what to say."

She reached for his hand, gripping it tightly. "I'm happy to be there, and I'm sure you'll figure out what to say. But you also may need to think about getting a DNA test or something. How else will you know for sure she's your birth mother?"

He stared at their clasped hands for a long moment before meeting her gaze. "DNA results take a while."

Was he thinking of celebrating the holiday with this woman? Megan thought it might be a good thing if he did, since he lost his wife and son around the same time. Finding a mother might be the balance he needed.

"Well, let's hear what she has to say first. Maybe a DNA test won't be necessary."

"Maybe." He squeezed her hand. "Thanks."

For a moment their gazes caught and clung, emotion and awareness shimmering between them. Drake leaned forward as if he might kiss her again. She held her breath, waiting. Hoping.

The door banged open, startling her. She instinctively pulled her hand from his as Jenna entered the debriefing room.

"Brr. It's cold out there." Jenna shivered as she shrugged off her coat. "I can't wait until summer."

Summer. June. Baby. Megan forced a smile. "Me either."

"I'm not looking forward to taking my boards," Drake said wryly. "Although graduating and becoming a full-fledged doctor will be nice."

"See? Lots to look forward to." Jenna grinned.

"Like your wedding to Zane?" Megan teased.

"Yep, that too." Jenna swept past them to enter the lounge. They heard her gasp. "What in the world is that? A bedpan? On the top of a Christmas tree?"

She glanced at Drake, and they both cracked up.

"You can thank Kristin and Holt for that," Drake called out with a wide grin. "It was their idea."

Megan couldn't tear her gaze from Drake, his smile lit up his entire face making him look like a new man.

And more attractive than ever.

Had he really been about to kiss her again? Not likely. She reminded herself that they were friends. That he'd backed off after their hot kiss at her apartment. That he'd point-blank told her he wasn't ready for a relationship.

Yet deep down, she knew that it was already too late.

She cared about Drake, a lot. More than she should, considering she was at least twelve weeks pregnant with another man's baby.

What was wrong with her? The last thing she needed was a man to complicate her life. Besides, he would be finished with his Lifeline rotation after the first of the year.

Which was too bad as she was having trouble imagining her life without him.

～

THE FOLLOWING DAY, Drake sat in the living room of his barren condo, drinking coffee as he contemplated the idea of digging out the Christmas tree from the spare bedroom. Christmas was only five days away, so it seemed a little silly to bother with decorations at this point.

Today was the anniversary of his wife and son's passing. For weeks now, he'd dreaded this day, but when he woke up, his first thought wasn't about Serena or Lance.

Megan's smiling face had popped into his mind. Followed by the fact that he'd be seeing her soon as they drove down to Racine to meet the woman who might be his birth mother.

There were still twin aches deep in his heart for Serena and Lance. For the beautiful family he'd lost. For the bright future they'd never have. But somehow, his memories of them had turned sweet rather than bitter.

He'd loved them both more than anything. But life went on, and he had no choice but to move along with the rest of the world over these past twelve months.

Saving lives, the way God must want him to do.

It struck him that he'd made this arrangement to meet with Jolene Nevin on the same day he'd lost his family without even realizing it. Was that some sort of sign from God? Some way of the Lord showing him the path he should take?

Maybe.

It was probably better to be out and busy rather than sitting home to wallow in the past, the way he'd originally planned to spend the day. He'd purposefully arranged his schedule to have today off so he could grieve alone.

Driving to Racine with Megan hadn't been a part of the plan.

Yet as crazy as it sounded, he was looking forward to the day. To talking with Megan and holding her hand as he met with Jolene.

After draining his coffee, he set his mug aside and rose to his feet. No reason to pull the Christmas tree out of storage. He was working the holiday anyway. And he still remembered the painful process of taking off the decorations Serena had put up, removing the ornaments, and dismantling the tree.

He'd almost thrown everything out, but at the time, even that was too much work. Instead, he'd tossed everything into the large closet in the nursery and closed the door.

Maybe next year. For now, the creatively decorated Christmas tree at Lifeline was good enough for him. He smiled at the way Jenna had used white tape to create a star on the bottom of the bedpan in an effort to make the tree more festive.

He'd miss the Lifeline crew once he was finished with his rotation.

Megan most of all.

His chest tightened, and he told himself to shake it off. It wasn't as if he couldn't see her again, once he was back working in the ER at Trinity Medical Center. In fact, their schedules might end up being better aligned. The ED only did eight-hour stints, rather than twelve.

But they wouldn't be flying together any longer.

Okay, now he was getting all morose again. There was just enough time to stop at the cemetery to leave the flowers he'd purchased for Serena and Lance, then hit the gym before taking a shower. Exercise had worked to distract him in the past, surely it would work now.

Standing at the gravesite of his wife and son was difficult. He'd been there before, on their birthdays and his and Serena's anniversary. Yet he didn't feel the same sense of despair he'd felt three months ago.

A sign he was healing? Maybe. After turning away, he

headed for the gym. Exercise didn't work to take his mind off everything. He told himself that was only because he was conflicted about meeting Jolene. No matter how hard he tried, he couldn't imagine calling her *Mom*.

He arrived at Megan's apartment building thirty minutes earlier than planned. He pressed the buzzer, hoping she didn't mind.

"Yes?"

"It's Drake. I know I'm early, sorry."

"That's not a problem. Come on up." She pushed the button to release the lock so he could enter the building.

He took the stairs two at a time. Her apartment door was hanging ajar, but he knocked anyway, before poking his head in. "Megan?"

"I'll be there in a minute." Her voice was distant, as if she might be in the bathroom. He entered her cheery apartment, his gaze landing on the tree. He had to admit, it looked much better than the bedpan, catheter, IV tubing concoction they'd put together at Lifeline.

Maybe he should put up the stupid tree at his place, after all.

There was the loud whirring of a blow dryer. He went into the kitchen, searching for more coffee but only found tea. Feeling restless, he moved back into the living room.

Edging closer to the tree, he noticed a tiny helicopter ornament. One that looked amazingly like their Lifeline chopper. Seeing it made him smile.

"I knew you weren't really a grinch." Megan's voice came from behind him. He hadn't noticed the blow dryer had gone quiet.

He turned to look at her, his heart thumping crazily in his chest. As always, she was stunning, wearing her blond hair loose and wavy, the way he liked it. Like him, she was dressed casually in jeans and a sweater.

It took a moment to find his voice. "Really? You doubt me? After seeing my condo?"

She waved an impatient hand. "That's just because you haven't taken the time to decorate. We can do that later this afternoon if you'd like."

Decorate? With Megan? On the anniversary of his wife and son's deaths? He opened his mouth to refuse, but somehow the words came out differently. "Okay, we can do that."

Her smile widened, and it was all he could do not to take her into his arms to kiss her senseless. "Great. Are you sure you want to leave early?"

He tucked his hands into his pockets. "I couldn't stay home staring at my four walls a moment longer. It feels surreal to think I may be meeting my birth mother."

Her smile softened. "I'm sure it's not easy. Did you bring anything? Like a birth certificate?"

"No, I'm not even sure what my plan should be. Quiz her on my birth details to see if she passes the test?"

She wrinkled her nose. "Probably not the best way to start. You might want to simply ask why she believes she's your birth mother. Let her do the talking."

"Yeah, that sounds good." Just being with Megan helped him feel better. "We may as well hit the road. I'd rather get there early than sit around."

"Okay. Let me get my coat."

Less than five minutes later, they were in his car, heading toward the interstate. Megan fiddled with his radio until she found a station playing Christmas music.

"I still think it's strange that your birth mother is living in Racine just miles away from you." She glanced at him. "I guess when I think of adoptions, I think of kids being taken across state lines, maybe even halfway across the country. Not being right here in the same area of the state."

He nodded thoughtfully. "Yes, but if you think about it, there are likely plenty of kids being adopted from around here. Milwaukee isn't as big as Chicago, but it's not small either."

"True." She fell silent for several miles. "Drake?"

"Hmm?" He glanced at her.

"I'm glad you're not spending the day alone." She reached over to take his hand.

"You know what today is?" He was surprised because he hadn't shared the exact date of Serena and Lance's deaths with her.

"Yes. Don't be mad, but I looked it up."

He should have figured she would do something like that. Yet surprisingly, he wasn't upset. "I'm not mad."

"Good." She settled back in her seat without letting go of his hand.

The drive to Racine didn't take nearly as long as he'd anticipated. He found the Coffee Clutch Café without difficulty and pulled into the lot. They were a good twenty minutes early, but he figured they might as well head inside to get a seat.

He went around to help Megan out, keeping a hand under her elbow as the parking lot had some slippery spots. The wind was brisk, nearly tearing the door from his hands as he opened it for her.

"Whew," Megan said once they were safely inside. "You know what sounds good right now? Hot chocolate."

"Two hot chocolate's coming up." He moved forward to place the order.

When he had the two cups of steaming chocolate

topped with whipped cream, he scanned the small dining area. His gaze stumbled across a woman with dark hair seated near the fireplace. When she looked at him, he knew it was her.

Jolene Nevin.

His mother.

For a long moment, he couldn't move. Megan must have noticed her, too, because she gently nudged him forward.

"A-are you Drake Thorton?" The woman's voice wavered a bit, displaying her nervousness.

Somehow he managed to respond. "Yes, I'm Drake, and this is my friend Megan Hoffman. You must be Jolene."

"Yes." The woman stared at him with dark brown eyes that were just like his.

Lots of people had dark brown eyes. And dark brown hair. But her facial features were very similar to his.

Or maybe that was just wishful thinking on his part.

He set the hot chocolate down on the table before he dropped it.

"You're early." He pulled out a chair for Megan, then took the seat beside her.

Jolene flashed a smile. "So are you."

A long silence hung between them. He tried to think of something to say, but seeing Jolene in flesh and blood had knocked him for a loop.

"It's great to meet you," Megan said, breaking the silence.

"Likewise." Jolene dropped her gaze for a moment, then lifted her chin. "I suppose you want to know what happened twenty-eight years ago."

He managed to nod.

"As you probably guessed, I got pregnant in high school. My parents—well, let's just say they were horrified by my indiscretion. The father of the baby wanted nothing to do with me, and his parents obliged by whisking him off to college. They gave me money for an abortion, but I couldn't do it."

His gut clenched at the situation she was describing. It was worse than he'd imagined. "I'm sorry."

A faint smile tipped her lips. "I'm not sorry I had you, Drake. I'm only sorry I caved to the pressure of giving you up for adoption. My parents convinced me that William and Gretchen would be wonderful parents."

"You—knew them?" He hadn't anticipated that.

"Yes, they were with me the last trimester of my pregnancy, even stayed in the hospital with me when I gave birth." Her voice wobbled again. "You were a beautiful baby. Giving you away was the hardest thing I've ever done."

He stared at her, his mind whirling. Was Jolene being honest with him? Had she really known his parents?

Or was this some sort of trick?

Heaven help him, he couldn't say for sure.

12

D rake's dark brown eyes were filled with a wary confusion. Megan empathized with what he must be going through and reached over to take his hand, holding on to it beneath the table. He gripped her tightly as if desperately clinging to the connection between them.

When it appeared neither of them were planning to say anything more, she decided to ask a few questions. "Since you knew Drake's parents, I'm surprised they didn't tell him all about you." She glanced at Drake, remembering the story he'd told about his adoptive parents getting a divorce and shuttling him between them, without either fighting for sole custody. A child's memories couldn't be counted on for a 100 percent accuracy, but still she knew that their treatment of him had hurt. "Your parents didn't keep your adoption a secret, right? So there would be no reason for them to hide something like that."

Drake slowly shook his head. "No, it wasn't a secret. You raise a good question."

"It was my fault," Jolene confessed, staring down at her untouched coffee. "I told them I wanted to be anonymous."

"Why?" Megan could see some similarities between Jolene's and Drake's facial features, but that alone wasn't enough. She felt protective of him. So far, she wasn't getting the feeling this woman was out for money, but she didn't fully trust her either.

"That's a fair question," Jolene admitted. She blew out a breath. "Being pregnant so young, I thought I'd rest easy knowing my baby, my son was in good hands with two adoring parents. Something I couldn't give him. What could I do at sixteen? Drop out of school? Work a series of low-paying jobs?"

Megan understood where she was coming from.

"I'd planned to move on with my life, leaving everything behind." The woman gripped her cup so tightly Megan feared she'd crush it, sending hot liquid all over the table. "And I did, for a while. I went to college, became a registered nurse, fell in love, and got married." The ghost of a smile flitted across her features. "It was great, but when I became pregnant again, those long-buried memories came tumbling back." She finally lifted her gaze. "You never forget having a child. Never."

There was a long silence, and Megan knew she was right. Even just being twelve weeks along, she'd never forget this baby.

Drake cleared his throat. "How many children do you have?"

"Three, counting you. Two boys and a girl." Her smile faded. "As blessed as I am with my two children, I couldn't seem to get you out of my mind."

"Does your husband know about Drake?" Megan asked gently.

"Yes, of course." Jolene looked surprised. "I wouldn't lie to him. But when I mentioned finding you, Harper wasn't happy. He told me that disrupting your life wasn't my choice to make. But then I saw your post on Find Your Family and knew the time was right."

"If I ask my adoptive parents about you, what will they say?" Drake's question sounded a bit like a challenge, and she couldn't blame him. But hearing the truth from his parents would be easier and quicker than obtaining a DNA test.

"I imagine they'll explain how they worked with an adoption agency, met me, and decided to adopt you when you were born." Jolene didn't hesitate. "I'm sure they have paperwork of some kind related to all of this."

Drake glanced at Megan, and she gave a brief nod. It seemed reasonable to talk to his adoptive parents as a next step, and she prayed they'd cooperate with him.

"Where do your parents live now?" Jolene asked. "They used to live on The Hill."

That question appeared to jolt Drake. "My dad still does, but my mother lives in Burlington."

Jolene frowned. "You mean—they're divorced?"

"Yeah, and happily married to other people," Drake explained.

Megan watched Jolene closely. She looked upset at finding out the perfect life she'd imagined for her son hadn't come to fruition. "W-when?"

"I was about five when they split up and bounced back and forth between households until I left for college." Drake's tone was matter-of-fact when Megan knew there was a deep emotional scarring underneath.

"I had no idea." Jolene glanced away, brushing at her eyes. Megan felt certain in that moment that this woman was indeed Drake's birth mother. Who else would cry over a divorce? She felt certain adoptive parents had the same marriage stressors as those who had natural children.

"It's okay," Drake said, awkwardly offering comfort. "I'm fine."

It took a moment for Jolene to get a grip on her emotions. "Is that why you posted a message seeking your birth mother on the Find Your Family website?" she finally asked. "Because of the divorce?"

Drake shifted uncomfortably in his seat. "Not exactly. I was thinking more along the lines of learning more about your medical history and that of your parents."

"I see." Jolene nodded as if that made perfect sense. Megan continued to hold Drake's hand, offering support. "The good news is that my parents are still alive and very healthy. My dad had a cardiac cath and a stent placed for a blocked artery about a year ago, but no complications since."

Megan thought it was interesting that Jolene was a nurse and Drake had ended up going to medical school. Maybe he'd gotten the science gene from his mother.

Drake took a sip of his hot chocolate. "I don't suppose you know much about my biological father."

Jolene grimaced. "No, I'm sorry. Last I heard he lives in California now."

Drake nodded but didn't look too disappointed. Megan felt certain he'd gotten what he'd been looking for, whether he realized it or not.

Drake may have initiated contact through the site under the guise of searching for a medical history, but she felt certain there was more to it. Having a family of his own had likely spurred more curiosity about the woman who'd given him up for adoption. Losing his wife and son had been horrible, but Jolene represented a potential blessing. She was the family he might not realize he'd been looking for.

If he let his guard down long enough to embrace it.

"I want you to know I don't expect anything from you," Jolene said, breaking the silence. "I mean, I hope to keep talking to you, if you're interested, but I can understand if that's not what you want. Right now, I'm glad we had this chance to see each other. Meeting you, seeing the fine man you've grown into is enough."

"This—is a lot to take in," Drake admitted, glancing at Megan as if seeking help. "I'm glad we met today, too, but I'd like to talk to my parents before deciding anything else."

"I think that's a great idea," Megan chimed in. "There's no rush, right? Plenty of time to determine next steps."

"Of course." Jolene's smile betrayed a hint of sadness. "I appreciate you taking the time to come here today. Thanks for that, Drake."

"It was great meeting you too." Drake stood and gently tugged Megan to her feet. "Drive safe."

Jolene nodded, watching them go with a wistful expression etched on her features. Megan sensed her feelings were genuine but understood Drake's need to be cautious.

He didn't say anything as they got settled in the vehicle. Megan didn't push, knowing his mind was likely going in a million different directions.

"What did you think of her?" he asked, breaking the silence.

She glanced at him. "I think I should be asking you that question. She seemed honest and genuine to me, but your thoughts and feelings are all that matter."

Drake sighed. "I liked her, and it should be easy enough to verify her story."

She raised a brow, sensing there was more. "But?"

"But I'm not sure I want to get involved with her after today. Her father's cardiac issues aside, they seem relatively healthy, which is what I'd been concerned about. No need to get all friendly. After all, she has a husband and kids, a life of her own."

She frowned. "And you think she can't have a relationship with you because of that?"

He grimaced and shook his head. "I don't know. It might start out as seeing each other on occasion, but all too soon, she'll go back to being focused on her family and that will be that."

Her heart ached for him, for the little boy who'd been shuffled from one family to the other without ever really having a home. "Drake, just because your parents split up and didn't welcome you into their respective families doesn't mean that everyone else will do the same. Where there's love, there's always room for more. Don't shut her out without giving it a chance."

"Maybe." He didn't sound convinced, and she decided not to push.

Drake would have to come to terms with what he wanted out of life on his own. She couldn't do it for him.

And his instinct to shut others out was a big red flag to her burgeoning feelings toward him.

She might care about Drake, may even be falling for him, but she sensed that continuing down that path would only lead to heartbreak.

Placing a hand over her lower abdomen, she told herself to stay focused on what was important in her life.

Her child.

"ARE YOU HUNGRY FOR LUNCH?" Drake glanced at Megan, grateful she'd been there with him during the meeting with Jolene Nevin. Her presence had calmed him, just like when they flew together on the Lifeline helicopter. "We didn't get to finish our hot chocolate."

"I could eat," she agreed. "I've noticed that I feel sick when I'm hungry. Must be the baby's way of letting me know he or she is hungry too."

He smiled and gestured to a passing sign. "There's a nice Italian place if you're interested." He paused, then added, "Unless you think it might give you heartburn."

"Thankfully, I've discovered Tums work like a charm, so Italian sounds good to me."

He nodded and took the next exit toward the restaurant. Spending time with Megan felt natural, and for once he didn't feel the need to be alone.

They arrived at the height of the lunch hour, but their hostess managed to snag a cozy table for two in the back. He barely glanced at the menu, having already decided on spaghetti and meatballs.

"So many choices," Megan said as their server set glasses of water on the table.

"And all spicy. You may need to buy stock in Tums," he teased.

"Don't I know it." Megan took a sip of her water, then closed her menu a minute later. "Okay, I'm set."

"What are you having?" Drake eyed her curiously.

"Spaghetti and meatballs."

He laughed. "Me too."

When their server came by and took their order, he thought it was ironic to be here like this, enjoying time with Megan on what he'd anticipated being a horrible and emotionally draining day.

A flash of guilt caught him off guard. Was this wrong? Shouldn't he be remembering his wife and son? He'd only spent about fifteen minutes at the cemetery earlier that morning. Was that enough?

"Hey, earth to Drake."

Megan's voice brought him out of his reverie. "I'm here."

"Your mind wasn't." Her smile was gentle. "I'm sure it's not easy to be here like this."

"To be honest, it feels good. I stopped by their graves earlier today but didn't feel like staying as long as I normally do." He shrugged, meeting her gaze. "I would have thought today would have been much harder to get through, but it's been better than I expected."

Her face bloomed in a smile that warmed his heart. She was so beautiful, so fresh and honest.

Don't forget pregnant, a tiny voice in the back of his mind whispered.

"That's great to hear, Drake. You certainly deserve to be happy."

Did he? It wasn't something he'd thought about over the past year. He'd been focused on working hard, doing his best to learn everything about emergency medicine and saving lives. But the goal of being happy hadn't entered his mind.

Yet here he was feeling content and maybe just a little bit at peace with his past.

Was this God's plan for him? Maybe.

"I can see a shadow of doubt in your eyes," she teased. "Trust me on this, you deserve to be happy. I know it's been a hard year, and I'm not trying to minimize your feelings. But I don't think God wants you to give up living your life. I feel certain he wants you to move forward."

He nodded slowly. "I'm starting to think so too."

Their meals didn't take long, even though the place was packed. The tangy tomato sauce had a bit of a kick, and he glanced at Megan. "We may need to stop on the way home for more Tums."

"Trust me, I have a whole bottle tucked in my purse," she confided.

That made him chuckle as he dug into his meal. The food was delicious, and he noticed Megan seemed to be enjoying it too. Despite the need for antacids.

They chatted about work and their upcoming holiday schedule.

When his phone rang, he considered letting it go to voice mail. Glancing at the screen, he inwardly groaned when he recognized Jared's number.

"This can't be good," he said, showing Megan the screen. "Jared, what's going on?"

"We're being hit by the flu and I need someone to cover night shift. I know it will cause you to go over your work hours, but I'm getting desperate. The staff are dropping like flies."

"I'll work tonight, no problem." He didn't mind bending the work-hour rule.

"Thanks. I need a pilot too. Reese and Dirk are both out sick."

"A pilot?" He glanced at Megan, unsure if she wanted Jared to know they were together.

She held out her hand, indicating he should hand over the phone.

"Hang on, Megan's right here." He gave her the phone.

"I can work tonight." She listened for a moment, then said, "Yes, I'll make sure to get some sleep. I'll be fine, Jared, I promise. See you later, then." She returned the device.

"Need anything else, Jared?"

"No." Jared sighed heavily. "I'm flying today and will likely need to fly again tomorrow, so I really appreciate you and Megan filling in tonight. Make sure she goes home to sleep for a bit, okay?"

"Will do. Later." He disconnected from the call and signaled for the check and to-go bags.

Megan sighed and leaned back in her chair. "Lunch was delicious, thanks, Drake. I feel bad we don't have time to put up your tree."

"It's not a big deal. I hope heartburn doesn't keep you from sleeping well this afternoon. Jared really wants to be sure you're well rested before our shift." He pulled his credit card out of his wallet and tucked it in the billfold.

"I'll be fine," she assured him.

"I trust you, Megan. You're a great pilot."

She blushed. "Someday I'll be as good as Reese. He's amazing."

"So are you." He held her gaze, hoping she would realize he was being serious.

"Thanks."

He drove her home and insisted on walking her up to the door. "I appreciate your support today," he said in a low voice. "It would have been difficult to meet Jolene on my own."

"Of course, Drake. I'm glad I could help." She lifted up on her tiptoes to press a kiss to his cheek.

The innocent gesture quickly turned into something more. He pulled her close and stared down into her light gray eyes, before capturing her mouth with his.

She instantly melted against him, kissing him back in a way that made his blood boil. Kissing Megan felt right.

And this time, he didn't want to stop.

13

D rake's kiss was everything she'd yearned for and
more. He kissed her as if she were the most
important woman on the planet. As if he'd never
let her go.

Why had she ever fallen for Cal? At the moment there
was absolutely no comparison.

Drake was a much better kisser by far.

When they finally came up for air, she rested her head
in the crook of his shoulder, breathing heavily, doing her
best to rein in her crazy hormones.

"Amazing," she murmured.

"Yeah." He held her close for another long moment
before releasing her. "Thanks for lunch and for being there
with my meeting with Jolene."

"Anytime, Drake."

He trailed the tip of his index finger down her cheek. "I
hate to say it, but I should go. You need to get some sleep
and so do I."

"I know." She tipped her head back to look into his dark
brown eyes. They were clear, without any hint of regret. She

smiled, glad that he wasn't putting distance between them the way he had the last time they'd kissed. "I'll see you at Lifeline, then."

"Yes." He gave her another quick kiss as if he didn't want to leave, but then stepped back so she could enter her apartment. "Later."

She forced herself to cross the threshold, closing and locking the door behind her. For a moment she rested there, fingering her tingling lips.

"Amazing," she said again, pushing away from the doorway. Enough mooning over the guy. Thankfully, she'd see him again soon.

Besides, she did need to rest up for the long twelve-hour shift ahead of her. Normally she didn't do naps; however, being pregnant changed that. These days, exhaustion was her constant companion. She fell asleep almost immediately and didn't wake up until her alarm went off at 1800 hours.

Yawning and stretching, she crawled out of bed. After a quick shower, she dressed in her Lifeline flight suit.

She ended up arriving at the Lifeline hangar a good twenty minutes before her shift. No one was around, the crew must be out on a flight. After placing her leftover spaghetti and meatballs in the pilot's room fridge, she went out to the debriefing area to check the satellite, taking note of the weather conditions.

Winds weren't too bad, but there was the threat of snow later that night. They'd have to keep an eye on that and the possibility of ice forming on the blades.

She heard the *whomp whomp whomp* of the chopper coming in just as Drake entered the room.

"Did you get some sleep?" he asked, heading for the coffeepot.

The smell of coffee still made her feel nauseated, but she did her best to ignore it. "I slept for five hours, it was great."

"Jealous," he said with a wry smile. His eyes met hers over the rim of his mug. "I didn't sleep much at all."

She blushed and turned toward the flight crew that had just come in. Jared looked exhausted, and she wondered how many flight hours he was logging these days. Kate was with him, as was Dirk, their pilot.

"Thanks for coming in," Jared said with a tired smile. "Jenna should be here too. It's been great the way everyone has been pulling together to cover these shifts."

"Of course, it's the least we can do." Megan shifted her gaze to Dirk. "Any issues?"

The older pilot shook his head. "Nope, she's good to go. It hasn't started snowing yet, but there are flurries in the forecast. We have plenty of de-icing fluid in the tank, Mitch filled it up a couple of days ago."

She nodded and shifted her gaze to Jared. "Any pending transfers?"

"Nope. Maybe you'll have a quiet night." He yawned widely. "I'm heading out but will be back in the morning."

When Jenna arrived a few minutes later, Kate and Dirk left as well. The sky outside was dark and would be for most of their shift.

Their pagers went off almost immediately. Megan didn't bother looking at the message, instead heading into the hangar to pull out the chopper.

Drake and Jenna soon joined her, and they all pulled on their respective helmets. "Call is a motor vehicle accident on the interstate, the most serious injury is that of an eight-year-old boy with a head injury."

"Got it. Let's go." She jumped into the pilot's seat and

started the engine. "Base, this is Lifeline, requesting permission to take off."

"Granted, Lifeline, you're good to go."

She lifted the bird off the landing pad, banking to the right so they could head out to the interstate. She tried not to worry about the child they were picking up, knowing the boy would be in good hands with Drake and Jenna.

The crash scene was farther out than she realized, a good twenty minutes from their hangar in the town of Ixonia. Still, it was easily visible from the air as several ambulances and police vehicles surrounded the vehicle involved. The law enforcement officers on scene shut the interstate down, providing plenty of room for her to land.

Drake and Jenna jumped out and grabbed the gurney. She kept the blades going while she waited. This was the hardest part of her job. The red and blue flashing lights were so bright she couldn't see much beyond them.

Minutes ticked by slowly giving her a bad feeling. Usually the crew was intent on getting their patient to the hospital ASAP. She craned her neck, trying to see better. Finally, she caught a glimpse of Drake and Jenna wheeling a gurney toward the chopper.

It didn't take long for them to get the gurney inside. "We need to take him to Children's Memorial," Drake said through the microphone.

"Will do." She requested permission and listened as Jenna and Drake worked on the little boy.

And sent up a silent prayer for God to watch over the injured child.

"PULSE CONTINUES TO BE TACHY," Jenna said with urgency. "And his right pupil is still larger than the left."

Drake knew the kid's condition was tenuous. Benjamin Burke had been in his booster seat, but his side of the vehicle had been crushed up against the tree. He and Jenna had been forced to wait for the paramedics to use the jaws of life to extricate him from the vehicle.

Long agonizing minutes.

"Keep the cooling protocol going." His main concern right now was Benjamin's head injury, but he still needed to do a full assessment, an impossible task to complete at the side of the road.

Drake noticed an abrasion along the left side of Benjamin's chest. Gently palpating the area, he felt certain the boy had sustained a couple of fractured ribs. He was glad the child was unconscious and unable to experience any pain from those ribs.

Staying along his left side, he checked the boy's upper extremity. His left wrist looked swollen, maybe a sprain or a fracture, so he quickly applied a splint.

"Drake? His IV blew."

"Get me a central line." He couldn't blame the paramedics for placing a peripheral IV, it was all they could accomplish while the kid was pinned inside the vehicle.

Jenna opened the kit, and he quickly prepped the right side of the boy's chest, staying away from his injured side. Placing a central line wasn't easy in a child, but he'd done it before and prayed God would guide him in doing so again.

"Got it," Jenna said with satisfaction when the blood flashed through the connection.

"Yeah." He sutured the line in place, then moved out of the way so Jenna could place a dressing over the site.

When that task was complete, he went back to his

assessment. The kid's belly was soft, which was a relief. No sign of intra-abdominal bleeding. He moved lower, then sucked in a harsh breath.

"What is it?" Jenna asked with concern.

"His left leg." The limb was extremely swollen to the point he wondered how he hadn't noticed until now. He tried to feel for a pulse behind the boy's knee and in his foot.

Nothing.

His gut clenched, and he glanced at Jenna. "He has compartment syndrome. Megan? What's our ETA?"

"Twelve minutes."

Going that long without a pulse was not acceptable. He swallowed hard. "I need drapes, sterile gloves, antimicrobial solution, and a scalpel."

"What are you going to do?" Jenna rummaged in their flight bag for the proper supplies.

"He needs a fasciotomy." Something he'd only watched being done but had never performed, especially not on a child.

"Are you sure?" Jenna's tone held doubt, even though she quickly opened the supplies he'd requested.

"Drake? Do you need me to divert to another hospital?" Megan asked with concern.

"No. He'll get the best care at Children's Memorial." He met Jenna's grim gaze. "I need the gloves first while you drape the leg."

She nodded and did as he requested. The interior of the helicopter wasn't sterile, but he was determined to do his best to prep the kid's leg.

"Scalpel," he said to Jenna.

She carefully opened the package so he could grab it while maintaining sterility. Taking a deep breath and willing his fingers to remain steady, he began to make several long incisions in the child's leg.

Jenna pulled dressings out of the bag as the wounds began to bleed. He felt bad about the scarring that would result, but releasing the pressure on the muscles by opening the hard and compact tissue was the only way to save the leg. He couldn't bear the thought of this child suffering an amputation.

Better to have scars than a prosthesis.

"Check his popliteal pulse," he said when he'd finished the last long incision.

Jenna gently lifted the leg, sliding her gloved hand beneath the bend in his knee. She lifted her gaze to his, reflecting admiration. "It's faint, but it's there."

"Good." He placed the scalpel in a sharps container and then changed his gloves to assist with dressing the wounds. Megan sent the chopper into a wide curve, no doubt heading down to the landing pad of Children's Memorial.

He was dizzy with relief when Megan landed the chopper gently on the rooftop landing pad. He finished wrapping the boy's injured leg in an ace wrap, even knowing the medical team inside would need to replace it, then tucked the cooling blanket over him.

"You first," Jenna suggested.

He nodded, jumped down, and ran to the back hatch. After pulling out the gurney, she joined him so they could wheel Benjamin inside.

When they arrived in the ED, he quickly informed the attending on duty what had transpired. "Severe case of compartment syndrome in his left leg, likely related to a crush injury at the scene. I'm not a surgeon but felt it was necessary to perform a fasciotomy en route."

"Gutsy move." The attending's expression was thoughtful as he unwrapped and examined Benjamin's leg. Drake felt himself holding his breath as the provider felt for a pulse. What if Jenna had imagined it? What if this poor kid loses his leg after all? He wasn't a surgeon, and for all he knew, he could have caused more harm than good in his efforts to help.

"Pulses are plus two." The provider met his gaze and nodded. "Nicely done."

He managed to find his voice. "Thank you."

"How's his head injury?" The provider gestured for one of the nurses to wrap the kid's leg as he shifted his attention to the boy's neuro status.

"Left pupil is larger than the right. We've been cooling him during transport," Jenna said as she began disconnecting the boy from their Lifeline portable monitors. Drake pitched in to help while the ER nurses began reconnecting him to their equipment.

"Hmm." The attending examined the boy's pupils for himself and nodded. "They're not that far off now, looks as if the cooling protocol is working."

Drake and Jenna helped scoot the boy over to the ED hospital gurney. When they had all their own equipment wiped down with bleach and piled on their transport gurney, they were ready to go.

When they reached the hallway, Jenna flashed a grin. "I can't believe you actually performed a surgical procedure on that kid."

"I know, it was crazy, but necessary." He hit the elevator button.

"How did you know what to do?" Jenna pushed the gurney into the open elevator.

"I've watched it being done in the ER by the trauma

surgeons. Thankfully, there isn't a lot of actual surgical technique involved."

"Still, I'm sure it wasn't easy."

"No, it wasn't." Good thing she hadn't noticed how his fingers had trembled while wielding the scalpel. Obviously, a career as a surgeon was not in his future.

When they reached the rooftop landing pad, they took a moment to don their helmets before approaching the whirling blades of the helicopter. Drake ducked as he slid the gurney in through the back hatch, before jogging over to climb in after it.

He connected his helmet to the intercom. "We're ready when you are, Megan."

"How's the little guy?" she asked.

"Doing much better thanks to Drake," Jenna said, playfully smacking him on the arm. "I have to say, watching you do that fasciotomy was a first for me and very educational."

Drake felt embarrassed with all the attention. "It's part of the job."

"I'm glad he's okay. Listen, we just received a request to fly to Appleton for an ICU to ICU transfer," Megan informed them. "The call came in while you were getting settled back there. I need to know from you if we should leave from here or head back to the hangar for supplies."

Before he could respond, their respective pagers went off. Drake read the message on the screen. "Fifty-one-year-old female in full-blown septic shock and on vasopressors. They're requesting a transfer to Trinity Medical Center. Jenna, what's your take on the supplies?"

"We're good, only used pediatric ones during the last transfer."

He nodded. "Megan, what do you think? Do we have enough fuel to fly to Appleton and back?"

"Yes. And the weather conditions are predicted to be good for the next few hours, nothing but snow flurries in our future. That puts us in green flying conditions."

Jenna sat back in her seat with a grin. "At least a trip north will make the night shift go by faster."

"I agree," Drake said. "Okay, Megan, let's go."

"Sounds good." Megan connected with the paramedic base, coordinating a flight path.

Five minutes later, the chopper went airborne. He smiled remembering how exciting his first flight had been. Now it was almost commonplace.

A weird light in the sky to the right side of the chopper caught his eye. Frowning, he leaned forward, then cued his mic. "Megan? Do you see that weird light out there?"

"Where?" The moment she asked, there was a loud clanking noise. The helicopter abruptly lurched sideways, then Megan's voice came through his headset. "Mayday, mayday, we've suffered a drone strike. Repeat, drone strike. Going down for a hard landing."

Hard landing? Drake felt his mouth go dry as the chopper tilted, sending him off balance.

They were going to crash!

14

Megan fought hard to keep the chopper level. If one of the rotators hit the building or the ground, they'd spin out of control and crash.

Please, Lord, help me!

The bird still lurched to the right as if the stupid drone had damaged one of the blades. "Come on, come on," she muttered, using all her strength to force the stick over while descending to the landing pad.

The lights lining the roof flashed in her peripheral vision. She didn't dare take her eyes off the instrument panel, knowing they were close.

So close.

There! The concrete landing pad was only a few yards below them. She dropped the chopper lower until they hit with a loud thud.

The bird lurched to the side as one of the struts broke. In a quick move, she shut down the engine. The blades slowly stopped spinning, and the chopper stayed put.

Safe. Dear Lord, they were safe.

Still gripping the stick, Megan dropped her chin to her chest and closed her eyes.

The worst landing she'd performed while stateside. Sure, she'd had some tough situations while trying to land amidst the rocky terrain of foreign countries, but nothing like this.

All because of a stupid drone. The minute she'd heard Drake mention the lights, she'd known.

People who flew drones were not supposed to be anywhere near air space—like helicopter landing pads. And they required special licenses to fly the drones at night.

And for what? Kicks and giggles?

"Lifeline, this is paramedic base. Are you okay? Over."

She forced herself to unclench her fingers from the stick long enough to hit the intercom switch. "Base, this is Lifeline. We've landed at Children's Memorial, but the helicopter is damaged. Repeat, the chopper is damaged. We are unable to fly, over."

"Roger, Lifeline, we'll let Appleton know another transport will be required."

She flipped off the switch and reached for the clasp on her harness. Her door wrenched open, a cold blast of air hitting her face. Drake's features filled her line of vision.

"Megan? Are you okay?"

"Yes. You? Jenna?" Her voice sounded hoarse, as if she'd been screaming.

Maybe she had.

"We're fine." Drake gently pulled her out of the seat, down onto her feet. Just having him close helped keep her steady. "Let's get inside."

"Okay." Her voice sounded muffled as if at the end of a long tunnel. It took her a moment to remember she still wore her helmet. She pulled it off and tucked it under her arm.

As Drake led her inside, she got a closer look at the chopper leaning to one side, its belly resting against the concrete landing pad. It looked like a giant beetle missing one side of its legs.

They weren't flying anywhere tonight. Or in the near future.

Guilt hit hard. Not only had she crashed the chopper, but there was a sick patient up in Appleton expecting them to come transport her to a higher level of care. What if that lady died because of her?

What if the entire crew had perished?

Her knees went weak, forcing her to lean against Drake to remain upright. As soon as they got inside the lobby area where the elevator was located, she stopped and braced a hand against the wall.

"I need to call Jared." It was the first thing she could think of. Jared needed to know how badly she'd damaged the helicopter.

"Plenty of time for that later. Let's head to the cafeteria to sit down for a while." The way Drake hovered at her side made her realize she must look about as bad as she felt.

The poor guy was always seeing her at her worst.

"I'd rather go back to the Lifeline hangar." Sitting in the hospital cafeteria with people surrounding them was not at all appealing.

Jenna and Drake exchanged a glance. "Okay, we'll walk back to Lifeline," Jenna agreed.

"Wait." She held up a hand. "What about the chopper? I can't just leave it sitting out there."

"Well, you can't fly it," Drake pointed out. "When we get

to Lifeline, we'll see if Mitch can come and take a look at it yet tonight."

It went against every instinct to leave the broken chopper behind, but she knew Drake was right. She couldn't fly it. Not when she had no idea how much damage had been done by the drone.

"I'd like to report that drone to the FAA," she said as they took the elevator down to the main level.

"Are you sure it was a drone?" Jenna asked.

She glanced at Drake. "You saw the lights, didn't you?"

He nodded slowly. "Yes, three small lights in a row hovering in the air, much like those old UFOs people talked about in the early seventies."

"I'm sure it was a drone. We've had trouble with them before. A special license is required to fly them, and per the FAA, all drone owners are also supposed to stay out of air space. There's no way that drone should have been so close to the landing pad at Children's Memorial."

"Why do they bother flying drones at night?" Jenna asked, her brow furrowed in confusion. "You'd think they'd stick to daytime hours."

"Photos, I guess, and there was a lot of news about how the rules were changing to allow special licenses for drone owners who wanted to fly at night." She sighed and rubbed her temple. "I should have seen it earlier and found a way to avoid it."

"It was behind your line of vision, Megan," Drake said.

She shook her head without saying anything more. The crash landing had been rough. Placing a hand over her lower abdomen, she swallowed hard. Thankfully, everyone was okay, this time.

But she couldn't help but wonder if a better pilot, one

like Reese, would have found a way to land the chopper without damaging it the way she had.

DRAKE WAS MORE RATTLED by the landing than he wanted to admit. Sure, they'd all walked away this time, but there was always a risk with flying.

Megan would be a Lifeline pilot long after he was back finishing up his emergency medicine residency.

The idea of losing Megan and her unborn child brought back memories of the motor vehicle crash that had taken Serena and Lance. This was why he'd wanted to stay far away from becoming involved.

He couldn't do this again. He couldn't love someone and lose them again.

When they reached the Lifeline hangar, Megan disappeared inside the pilot's room presumably to call Jared and Mitch. He dropped onto the edge of the sofa next to Jenna.

"That was a close one," Jenna said.

He nodded but didn't say anything. The reality of their near miss was still messing with his head.

"I need to call Zane." Jenna surged to her feet, pulling her cell phone from her pocket. "Just in case he somehow hears about this through the grapevine."

He scrubbed his hands over his face. Without a chopper, he didn't see a reason to stick around. No sense in getting paid to sit here and do nothing for the rest of the night.

Would Jared shut Lifeline down temporarily? By the time Mitch was able to repair the chopper, his rotation here could very well be over.

"I spoke to Jared," Megan said upon entering the lounge. "There's a second helicopter being stored at a local airport.

Jared is making arrangements to get it here sometime tomorrow. In the meantime, we can all head home. Mitch will go to Children's Memorial tonight, pull the chopper out of the way, then return to work on the bird first thing in the morning."

He nodded and rose to his feet. "I'll walk you out to your car."

"No need. I have to finish my crash report. The FAA requires one to be completed within twenty-four hours of the event."

He hesitated, thinking he should offer to stay, yet needing some distance. He'd kissed her twice, but now he wanted nothing more than to finish his Lifeline rotation and move on.

He couldn't do this again.

Megan stared at him for a long moment, then turned and walked away.

He didn't call her back. Instead, he walked Jenna out to her car, then drove home to his condo.

It was sterile and empty as always, yet somehow it bothered him now. He sensed Serena would be upset that he hadn't decorated for Christmas. That he didn't have family photos displayed prominently on the mantel above the fireplace.

His chest squeezed with pressure, and he put a hand over his heart as if that might ease the tension.

It didn't.

Why this sudden preoccupation with the near crash? Megan's job was no more dangerous than anyone else's. She wasn't in the military any longer, and she wasn't in law enforcement. But that moment when he opened her door and saw her bent over, he'd thought the worst. That she'd been hurt.

She wasn't. And that was something to be thankful for.

So why was he sitting here alone in the dark rather than calling her?

He had no idea.

MEGAN KNEW something was wrong with Drake but needed to focus on salvaging her career. While she didn't think Jared would fire her for a drone strike, she knew the FAA would investigate.

And she needed to be prepared.

Sure enough, the following morning the FAA representatives arrived at Lifeline to question her about the sequence of events that had transpired that fateful night.

She only saw Drake in passing, he hadn't called or checked in on her. The closeness they'd once shared had evaporated in an instant.

His lack of contact stung, but she did her best to ignore it. By the third day post crash landing, she was cleared of any wrongdoing and released to return to work. Just in time to take over her Christmas Eve holiday shift.

She mentally braced herself for seeing Drake. It was possible he'd found someone to switch shifts with him, but unlikely considering it was the holiday. Everyone else likely had plans to spend the evening with their families.

Drake wasn't there when she arrived, but the night crew was all huddled around the table in the debriefing room. The replacement chopper had been up and running for a few days now, and the flu bug seemed to have run its course.

Reese was sitting beside Kate and Matt, his gaze zeroing in on her when she dropped into the seat beside him.

"How are you?" His expression was full of concern.

She forced a smile. "I'm fine, thanks."

"I had a similar experience earlier this year, a crash landing in February when Samantha's ex shot at the bird while we were in flight." He reached over to rest his hand on her shoulder. "I know how difficult it is getting through something like that."

"Thanks." It meant a lot coming from someone who'd been there. "I only wish I'd have seen the drone sooner."

Reese's gaze darkened. "That idiot shouldn't be flying the stupid thing so close to the helipad."

"I know. Thankfully, the FAA has a line on the person involved." It was the only good news to come out of the past few days. "They're issuing a hefty fine and holding them responsible for the chopper repairs."

"Good. I hope this helps reinforce the rules for everyone else owning and operating a drone." Reese gently squeezed her shoulder, then turned toward the radar screen. "Snow in the forecast for today. Although there are only flurries now, that could easily change. You'll want to keep an eye on the weather conditions. I placed us in yellow flying status for now. Only responding to trauma calls within a twenty-mile radius."

"Sounds good."

Drake entered the hangar, bringing a cold gust of air with him. She glanced at him, but he avoided her gaze. "Sorry I'm late."

So this is how it was going to be? Great. Just Great.

"Who are you flying with?" Matt asked.

"Me. I'm here." Jessica came in right behind Drake. Jessica worked only part time and was required to do two holiday shifts.

"There's a pending transfer from Racine," Matt said once Jessica was seated beside Drake. "Reese has had us in yellow flying conditions, so we have the transfer on hold. They're considering ambulance options."

"Yellow conditions?" Drake's gaze skittered past her to Reese.

"It's snowing, and the winds are supposed to pick up. That can cause ice to form on the chopper blades. We're down one chopper, so for now, we're yellow."

"Got it," Jessica said. "Racine should just go with the ambulance, it's less risky than waiting for a change in the weather."

Matt nodded and yawned. "That's it for us, right, Kate?" When the flight nurse nodded, he stood. "We're outta here."

Megan stayed in her seat near the radar screen as the rest of the crew filed out. Ridiculous tears pricked her eyes. She decided to blame her hormones.

Drake must have thought she was a terrible pilot. It's the only thing that made sense as to why he'd so abruptly withdrawn from her. He was so kind and caring immediately after their crash landing, but now he wouldn't even meet her gaze.

Much less call.

Jared, the FAA investigators, and Reese didn't blame her, but Drake did. How ironic was that?

She took note of the change in wind speed, heading toward thirty-five miles an hour. Combined with the increase in snow, their conditions would soon be red.

Which meant sitting around for the next twelve hours.

Deciding to heat more water for tea, she turned just as Drake was coming back inside to get coffee. For a long moment, they stood staring at each other.

"Um, the Racine transfer is off, they went with ground transport instead." Drake stuffed his hands into the pockets of his flight suit. "Thought you should know."

"Well, don't worry, you don't have to risk flying with me, I'm declaring red flying conditions. The wind is coming in at thirty-five miles per hour. Combined with snow makes for poor flying conditions."

"I'm not worried about flying with you." He looked surprised at her statement.

"Sure, that's why you've been radio silent these past three days." She couldn't hide the sarcasm.

He reached up and rubbed the back of his neck. "It's not that. It's—that was a close call. I kept thinking about how I lost Serena and Lance . . ." His voice trailed off.

She blinked. Seriously? That's what this was about? She took a step toward him. "Drake, you have to know that flying isn't nearly as dangerous as driving. There are by far more car crashes each year than helicopter or plane crashes."

He looked away, shrugged. "Yeah, I know."

Her heart squeezed in her chest. Of course he knew, he'd lost his family in a car crash. She gave herself a mental head-slap. Taking a deep breath, she edged closer until she could reach out and touch his arm. "You've been through a very difficult time, Drake. I'm sure it's not easy to let go of the people you loved. Your beautiful wife and son will always be a part of you, here in your heart." She tapped her finger against the center of his chest. "But you also can't live your life by constantly playing the what-if game. Life is too short. None of us are guaranteed tomorrow. All we can do is to put our faith and trust in God."

"I won't survive another loss." The words came out so soft she could barely hear them.

"I know you think that now, but that's not how life works. We don't get to make deals with God. Whatever the future holds, you'll get through it and so will I. It's part of having faith and trusting God's plan. As difficult as it's been for you, you must know your wife and son are in a better place in heaven. That wasn't what you wanted, but that was God's decision. We can't question His plan. All we can do is move forward."

He was silent for a long moment before reaching up to cover her hand with his, holding it tightly against his chest. "I know you're right, but going through that crash landing brought all my old fears and feelings to the forefront. It's been rough to get through."

"That's understandable, Drake. We're only human."

He stared deep into her eyes. "I've missed you, Megan. These last few days have been lonely without you."

Her heart melted. "I've missed you too." She had to blink back more tears. "I've fallen in love with you, Drake. I know I'm pregnant and that you could do so much better than me, but I love you. And I want you to be happy, so no pressure. If you aren't ready, that's fine. It's your decision on where to go from here."

"Love?" Her words appeared to have caught him completely off guard. "You—love me?"

"Yes." A kernel of sadness swirled in her gut. Just because she loved him didn't mean he felt the same way. But she wasn't going to back down now. "I love you. But I know this is a bad time, and there's no rush. Maybe in a year or so—"

"I love you too," he blurted, interrupting what she'd been about to say. He pulled her into his arms and hugged her close. "I love you, Megan. I didn't want to, frankly, I fought against it every step of the way, but somehow it happened anyway. You managed to wiggle your way into my heart."

"Gee, just what a woman wants to hear," she teased.

He sighed and tipped her chin up so he could look into

her eyes. He lightly brushed the pad of his thumb down her cheek. "Let me try that again. I love you, Megan. You and your baby. I know we've only been together for the past couple of weeks, and we don't have to decide anything today, but I believe God has brought us together for a reason. I'm begging you to give me another chance."

"I think I can manage that."

"Good." He pulled her closer and kissed her. When Jessica came in, they pulled apart.

"Oops, sorry." Jessica quickly retreated.

"I think God brought you into my life on purpose," Drake whispered.

"I'm sure of it," she agreed. "And I feel the same way."

"You should know I've been talking to Jolene a bit. We may get together after the holiday. I'd love for you to join us."

"Oh, Drake, that's wonderful news. I'm happy to come along."

"Great." He hugged her, then said, "Oh, one more thing. Do you think you'd have some time after our shift tonight to decorate my condo for Christmas?" Drake asked.

"I'd love to." She nestled against him for a moment, thinking about what a blessing this holiday turned out to be.

For both of them.

EPILOGUE

Six months later . . .

Drake had just finished his emergency medicine board exam when Megan's text came through.

I'm in labor.

They had a game plan in place just for this contingency. At least he'd already finished his boards and wasn't just starting them. No doubt Ivan was already in the process of driving Megan to Trinity Medical Center. He quickly texted her back.

On my way. Will meet you at the hospital.

Once he was behind the wheel, he used the hands-free function of his car to call Jolene, letting her know Megan was in labor. He, Megan, and Jolene had grown close over the past six months. He'd been honored Jolene and her husband, Harper, had attended his and Megan's Valentine's Day wedding.

The hospital wasn't far, only fifteen minutes away, but he pushed the speed limit anyway. No way was he missing a minute of his wife giving birth to their son or daughter.

They had a bet going. He was convinced the baby was a boy; Megan felt certain she was carrying a girl. Deep down, they didn't really care as long as the baby was healthy.

After parking in the first available spot he could find, he bolted inside the hospital heading directly to the labor and delivery unit. For a split second he thought about Serena and the son he'd lost, but then he caught a glimpse of Megan sitting in a wheelchair with Ivan Ames standing next to her.

"I'm glad I didn't miss much." He bent down to give Megan a kiss, then nodded at Ivan. "Appreciate the help, Ivan."

"Hey, it's no problem." Ivan grinned. "Sounds like pregnancy is contagious these days. Kate announced she and Ethan are expecting and so are Kristin and Holt. I'm sure it's only a matter of time before Jenna follows suit."

"Jenna and Zane just got married," Megan protested, grimacing as a contraction hit hard. She breathed through it for a long moment before adding, "Give them some time."

"Mrs. Thorton?" The nurse crossed over to the desk. "Dr. Whalen is on her way in to see you. I'm Natalie, your nurse for the rest of the evening." Natalie pushed her wheelchair down the hall, leaving Drake to follow. "You'll be going into room ten."

"Keep us posted," Ivan called. "If Megan has that baby today, Jared's in the running to win the pool."

Drake waved a hand acknowledging him. Jared and the rest of the Lifeline crew had a baby pool going as well, and dinner for the entire crew was on the line.

"Ooh, these contractions are strong," Megan said with a low groan as Natalie helped her get from the wheelchair into the bed.

"This is your first baby, right?" Natalie smiled gently. "The first ones usually take a while, but I'll do a quick exam once you're in a hospital gown to see how things look."

Drake stood nervously next to Megan's bed. "Everything's going to be fine."

"I know." Her face contorted in another grimace as she was gripped by another contraction. He frowned, thinking they were not only strong but coming pretty fast.

"You'd better check her now," he told Natalie. "Those were barely two minutes apart."

"In a moment." Natalie was helping remove Megan's clothes and slipping on a hospital gown.

He curled his fingers into his palms to keep from ripping the gown out of the way. He tried to remind himself he wasn't an OB expert and that he was here as the husband and father, not a doctor. But he found himself thinking if Natalie didn't get a move on, he'd shove her aside and check Megan's progress for himself.

"Oh my goodness. You're already eight centimeters dilated." Natalie's voice reflected surprise when she finally did the exam. "I'd better get Dr. Whalen in here."

"Yeah, you do that," Drake said before he could check himself.

"Relax, Drake, at least we're in the hospital and not at the side of the road," Megan teased.

He didn't want to remember the baby he'd delivered at the scene of a motor vehicle accident. Those brief seconds when the baby hadn't breathed haunted him still.

"Hello, Megan, Drake." Dr. Cindy Whalen breezed in. "I hear you're about to have a baby."

"I may have waited a little too long," Megan confessed, shooting him a guilty look. "Drake was taking his boards, and I was trying to hold off."

"Megan." He sighed and took her hand in his as another contraction hit.

"Things look good, Megan," Dr. Whalen assured them. "Baby's head is crowning, and you're fully dilated now. No time for an epidural or anything else, sorry. Right now you're going to have to concentrate on pushing for me, okay? As soon as the next contraction begins, I want you to push."

Drake couldn't believe it was happening so fast.

"Push," Dr. Whalen repeated.

Megan groaned and pushed, sweat dampening her temples. He helped support her with an arm around her shoulders but felt helpless and useless as Megan pushed.

"Good, we're almost there. On the next contraction, push again."

Megan didn't answer, all her concentration turned inward as she sought the strength to push their baby into the world.

"There! A beautiful baby girl! Congratulations, Mom, Dad." A second later, their daughter began to cry, showing off a healthy set of lungs.

"A girl." Megan smiled, tears glistening in her light gray eyes. Dr. Whalen wrapped a blanked around their daughter and nestled her against Megan's chest, maximizing skin to skin contact. "Look at how precious she is, Drake. We have a baby girl."

He had to blink away his own tears. "Yes," he managed, his voice hoarse with emotion. He kissed Megan's forehead and then his daughter's "Welcome to the family, Joy Ruth Thorton." Joy was for the way Megan had brought happiness into his world, and Ruth was Jolene's middle name.

"I love you, Drake." Megan gazed up at him, then back down at their daughter. "Thank you for making my life complete."

"I love you too." Joy might not be his daughter by blood, but she was his daughter by heart.

And that was all that mattered.

DEAR READER,

I hope you enjoyed Megan and Drake's Christmas story! *A Doctor's Christmas* is the sixth and last book in this series. I want to thank you for the kind notes and rave reviews about my Lifeline Air Rescue stories. I'm thrilled at how many of you have enjoyed reading about this exciting aspect to the medical profession.

Please know reviews are so important to authors. If you would take the time to review this book, I would be eternally grateful.

I adore hearing from my readers. I can be contacted via my website at https://www.laurascottbooks.com or on Facebook at https://www.facebook.com/LauraScottBooks or on Twitter at https://twitter.com/laurascottbooks. Also, please drop by my website to sign up for my newsletter, I offer a free novella that is not available for sale on any vendor site for all subscribers.

Lastly, if you haven't had a chance to read my McNally Family series, I've included the first chapter of *To Love* for you here.

Dear Reader,

Until next time,
Laura Scott

TO LOVE

Several loud thuds woke Jazzlyn McNally up from a sound sleep. For a minute, she thought the noise had been something she'd dreamed, then she heard it again. Louder. She wasn't sure, but it almost sounded as if several two-by-fours were being dropped.

What in the world?

She rolled out of bed, tugging her oversized T-shirt down over her gym shorts, and headed downstairs, wincing as one of the wooden boards creaked beneath her bare feet. What if the noise was from somewhere inside the house? She reached the bottom of the stairs, flattened herself against the wall, then gingerly peered around the corner, looking into the great room.

Casting her gaze over the main living area, the fireplace, the lighthouse oil painting over the mantle, and the antique glossy cherrywood furniture, nothing seemed out of place. But she knew she hadn't imagined the sounds, so as she made her way through her grandparents' old mansion, she picked up a claw hammer to use as a possible weapon.

Everything was fine inside the house, but when she

walked over to the French doors overlooking Lake Michigan, she noticed several boards strewn across the lawn.

Her gazebo!

Sick to her stomach, Jazz flung open the doors and stumbled outside.

No! It couldn't be! Two sections of the gazebo she'd worked on for the past three days had been destroyed in one fell swoop. She stared in horror, her mind trying to comprehend what had happened. Vandals had struck. In fact, the sledgehammer they'd used was still lying in the center of the destruction.

But who would do such a thing? And why?

In the early morning light, she could see the area was deserted. Whoever had done this was long gone. Maybe in the time it took her to go through the house. It was difficult to tear her gaze away from the damaged remnants of her hard work.

She shivered in the crisp April breeze coming off the lake. Drawing a deep shuddering breath, she turned and went back inside to find her cell phone. She called the Clark County Sheriff's Department for the second time in a week.

The first incident, a broken window in the front door, had been bad enough.

But this? Destroying two sections of the gazebo she'd recently repaired? This time, the vandals had gone too far.

"Clark County Sheriff's Department," the female dispatcher answered. "How can I help you?"

"This is Jazzlyn McNally, and I need a deputy here ASAP. The vandals have used my sledgehammer to wreck my gazebo; it's lying in pieces across my lawn."

"I'll send a deputy," the dispatcher responded. The

woman didn't ask for her address; the entire town knew where the McNally Mansion was located.

"Thank you." Jazz disconnected from the call and combed her fingers through her disheveled hair, her inner fury subsiding to a dull resignation. Even if the police found who'd done this, she would still need to fix everything that had been destroyed. At this rate, her goal of opening the B&B before Memorial Day wasn't going to happen.

She gave herself a mental shake, knowing she needed to remain positive. She could do this. How much time before the deputy arrived? She figured she had ten minutes at the most, so she ran upstairs to the green room, her favorite, to change into a sweatshirt and jeans.

Five minutes later, Jazz returned to the kitchen to brew a pot of coffee. The scent helped her to relax a bit, and she poured a cup, grateful for the jolt of caffeine.

But when the deputy still hadn't arrived by the time she'd finished two cups of coffee, her anger began to simmer. By eight o'clock in the morning, she tapped her foot on the floor, wondering how long it would take for someone to arrive.

Apparently, vandalism of personal property wasn't high on the Clark County Sheriff's list of priorities.

Another hour passed. A knock at the front door made her frown. She hadn't heard a car come up the driveway. Setting her coffee aside, she reached for her claw hammer and made her way to the newly repaired front door. She peeked through the recently replaced window.

A man roughly six feet tall with longish dark hair stood there, wearing a threadbare red and gray checkered flannel shirt, faded black jeans, and construction boots.

Not the deputy.

The vandal? But why knock at her door?

She hesitated so long he rapped again, a little louder this time. The stranger hunched his shoulders and rubbed his hands together as if he were cold. No car meant he'd either walked or hitchhiked from town.

Against her better judgment, she opened the door still holding the claw hammer in clear view as she eyed him with suspicion. "Yes?"

The stranger smiled, but it didn't reach his dark eyes. "Ms. McNally? My name is Dalton O'Brien, and I was told by Stuart Sewell from the hardware store that you might be looking for some construction help. I work hard and accept cash if you're interested."

Jazz stared at him for a long moment, wondering if this guy was really brazen enough to destroy her gazebo, then come back to ask to be paid to fix it. "How did you get here?"

He looked surprised at her question. "I hitched a ride from the Pine Cone Campsite. The driver let me out on Main Street, so I walked from there."

The Pine Cone Campsite was over twenty miles from the center of town. If he was being honest, then he probably wasn't her vandal.

Still, she didn't like the timing of his arrival.

"I can provide references if needed," O'Brien went on. "I did some work on Mrs. Cromwell's bathroom a week ago."

Jazz knew Betty Cromwell. Everyone in town knew Betty, the woman was one of the biggest sources of gossip in McNally Bay. If Betty would vouch for this guy, she may be interested.

She was just about to ask for his contact information when a dark brown sedan pulled in, the words Clark County Sheriff's Department etched along the side. Finally!

Dalton O'Brien turned to watch the cop car approach,

not looking the least bit nervous as he tucked his hands into the front pockets of his jeans.

Trusting her instincts wasn't easy. Jazz had learned the hard way that she was too naïve when it came to trusting men. Yet for some reason, she didn't think the handsome stranger was the person who'd vandalized her gazebo.

Or maybe she just didn't want to believe it.

"Ma'am, I'm Deputy Garth Lewis. I understand you've had more trouble this morning?"

"Yes." Jazz opened the door wider and gestured with her hand. "Come in, both of you. I have fresh coffee if you're interested."

Both Dalton and Deputy Lewis glanced around with interest. While she loved the beautiful great room, she led the way into the kitchen and pulled two coffee mugs out of the cabinet.

"O'Brien," Deputy Lewis said with a nod. "Are you here looking for work?"

"Yes, sir." Dalton didn't say anything more, and the two men stood awkwardly in the large kitchen.

It was reassuring that the deputy knew Dalton O'Brien by name. She handed them both steaming mugs of coffee. "Cream or sugar?"

"Black is fine," Deputy Lewis said.

"For me, too," Dalton added.

"Okay then. Mr. O'Brien, why don't you have a seat for a moment while I talk to the deputy?" She crossed over to the French doors, opened them, and then stepped back so the deputy could see the vandalism for himself.

Deputy Lewis let out a low whistle. "When did this happen?"

She crossed her arms over her Michigan State sweatshirt. "The noise woke me up at six this morning. I went through the house first, so I didn't see the damage out here right away. By the time I did, whoever had done this was long gone."

The deputy met her gaze. "I saw your report about the damaged front door and now this. Do you have any enemies that we need to know about?"

"None that I'm aware of." Jazz glanced at the stranger who'd come over to see the vandalism for himself. Then she turned back to the deputy. "You probably know this house belonged to my grandparents, Jerry and Joan McNally. Our family has lived here in Clark County for a hundred and fifty years, since our great-great-grandparents immigrated from Ireland. The bay was named after them."

"I'm well aware of the town history," Deputy Lewis said in a dry tone.

She gestured to the interior of the large Victorian house that she was in the process of turning into The McNallys' B&B. "My siblings and I only spent summers here, until our grandma passed away, willing the property to us. You'd know more about any possible enemies than I would."

"What's the approximate cost of the damage?" Deputy Lewis asked as he pulled out a small notepad and stubby pencil.

"Around two grand," the stranger said. "Maybe less, depending on how much of the lumber can be salvaged."

She stared at him in surprise. "That's exactly what I would have estimated," she murmured. "I guess you know your way around construction sites."

O'Brien gave a curt nod. "I do."

"Well then." Jazz let out her breath in a heavy sigh. "I guess I could use a little help, if you're willing."

The stranger nodded and took another sip of his coffee.

Jazz waited for Deputy Lewis to finish his report, which included taking pictures of the crime scene. He also bagged the sledgehammer, on the off chance he might be able to lift some fingerprints from the wooden handle. The deputy left, promising to be in touch if he had any news. Afterward, she returned to the kitchen, the stranger following like her shadow.

"You hungry?" she asked.

His eyes flared with hope. "Yes, ma'am."

"Please call me Jazz, ma'am makes me feel old. Veggie omelets okay?"

"I'm not picky," he said in a wry tone.

"Good." Jazz opened the fridge and pulled out a carton of eggs and the veggies—broccoli, onions, and mushrooms that were left over from the night before. "After breakfast, we'll get to work."

He nodded again without saying anything more.

A man of few words, she thought, his dark eyes shadowed with secrets. She told herself it didn't matter why he was hitching rides and living in a campsite. Not her business one way or the other.

Jazz only needed his assistance for the next couple of weeks, then he could be on his way. Fine with her, because she didn't need any complications in her life.

Or distractions.

IN DALTON'S OPINION, the veggie omelet Jazz had made for him was the best he'd ever tasted, but as usual, he kept his thoughts to himself.

He was only here to make a few extra bucks before moving on. His plan was to head farther north, knowing that construction jobs would be plentiful there during the summer months.

The damage to the gazebo made him mad, especially the way Jazz had looked so devastated at the senseless destruction.

Ms. McNally, he sternly reminded himself. Okay, yeah, she was beautiful with her long dark brown hair tousled from sleep, and her petite, curvy figure. The way she'd answered the door holding a claw hammer had made him smile, the image still burned into his memory. Beauty aside, he had no intention of crossing the line between employer and employee.

He was a drifter. As soon as this job was finished, he'd be on his way.

Truthfully, he was happy to help. He hated the idea of a young woman living in this huge rambling house alone while vandals went to town on her gazebo.

It wasn't right. He didn't know anything about the McNally legacy, since he'd only been in town for a couple of weeks now, but he had to agree with the deputy that the culprit must be someone holding a grudge against the family.

Which meant just about anyone in town could be considered a possible suspect.

Dalton finished his second cup of coffee, then carried his dirty dishes to the sink. "Thanks for breakfast," he said, then headed outside to see what he could salvage from the wreckage.

Not expecting to be put to work right away, Dalton had left his tool belt at the Pine Cone Campsite. He considered asking Jazz to drive him over there, then figured she probably had enough tools here for him to use.

By the time Jazz joined him, he'd picked through the

entire pile. The lumber he'd stacked together on the right side of the gazebo was good enough to be used again; the left side held the lumber split beyond repair.

"That's better than I'd hoped. This could come in closer to a thousand to repair, excluding labor."

"Agreed. If you're willing loan me tools, I'll begin construction."

"I don't have extras," Jazz said, her expression full of apology. "But you can use anything I have while I head out to buy more lumber."

"Or, if you don't mind swinging past the Pine Cone Campsite, I can pick up my tools," he offered. "We can get the lumber on the way back. With both of us working, we'll get this repaired in no time."

For the first time since he'd arrived, she broke into a wide smile. "Let's do it."

She was alarmingly stunning when she smiled, and he had to force himself to turn away. What was wrong with him? His wife Debbie and their young son, Davy, have only been gone eleven months, not even a full year. He wasn't about to try replacing them in his heart.

Not now. Not ever.

He followed Jazz through the old Victorian house to the circle drive out front. He hadn't paid much attention to the three-car garage, painted yellow with white trim to match the large house, but that's where Jazz headed.

Pushing numbers into a keypad, she stood and waited for the garage door to open. He wasn't sure why he expected to see a small compact car instead of the large bright blue Chevy pickup truck.

"Nice," he said, his tone full of appreciation. As soon as the words left his lips, he frowned. He didn't need a truck, or any other flashy items. That was part of a life he'd left behind and had no interest in returning to. All he needed was a tent, backpack, sleeping bag, and his tools.

"Thanks." Jazz didn't seem to notice anything amiss. She waited till he was seated beside her, before heading out of the garage, closing the door with the push of a button.

The ride to the campground didn't take long. Jazz followed his directions as he told her where to find his camping spot. The red tent was right where he'd left it. He slid out of the passenger seat and went over to unzip the front flap. His backpack, camping gear, and tools were tucked inside.

He emerged a few minutes later to find Jazz standing in front of his tent, regarding it thoughtfully. He lifted his construction tool belt. "I'm ready."

She nodded absently. "Do they charge you a fee to camp here?"

"Yeah, but it's nominal. Why?"

She bit her lower lip for a moment. "How would you feel about camping outside my place instead? It's free, and I'll throw in meals."

He shouldn't have been surprised, but he was. His first instinct was to refuse, he liked her too much already. But then he remembered the vandalism.

It wasn't his problem to keep her property safe. She'd notified the cops who would probably keep a close eye on things. Then again, he knew the deputies couldn't be there all the time. And if the vandals lived in town, they could be at the old Victorian and back within an hour.

"Never mind," Jazz said hastily as if sensing his reluctance. "It's a crazy idea."

Yeah, it was, but he nodded anyway. "I'll do it."

Her green eyes widened in surprise. "You will?"

"Yes. Although we haven't agreed on an hourly wage yet."

She named a fair sum, better than he'd hoped considering she was offering meals, too.

He took a step toward her and held out his hand. "Thank you. I'll take it."

She placed her small, yet slightly calloused hand in his, sending a sliver of awareness down his spine. He did his best to ignore it as they solemnly shook.

"It's a deal." She smiled again, stealing his breath. "I'll help you pack."

"No need, I have a system." He dropped her hand and stepped back, needing distance. He went to work dismantling his campsite with the ease of long practice.

After storing his items in the space behind the bench seat, he climbed in beside her, hoping he wasn't making a huge mistake.

Made in the USA
Monee, IL
09 September 2020